倍斯特出版事業有限公司
Best Publishing Ltd.

Jessica Su◎著

90關鍵商業烏龍句之
高效抓龍術
職場溝通不NG!

終結職場上的烏龍英語

辭不達意的原因在哪裡？ 沒有察覺到的錯誤英語話術有哪些？
【高效抓「龍」術】抓出各式烏龍用法，讓你說出**最道地的英文味**

生意成不成，關鍵在於**溝通話術**，
精準且正確的英文說法就是**成功的關鍵**！

本書規劃超過**90**句的常見英語烏龍句：
常見的文法、用字錯誤解析、延伸用語、正確的說法及完整的解析，
職場工作、生意往來**不詞窮**。

筆者有多年專職於與國際客戶交涉各式各樣商業問題的國貿經驗，遇過五花八門的
烏龍英語，以真實情境對話作為範例，除常見的文法遣詞上的錯誤，也涵蓋國人最常
犯的chinglish烏龍來撰寫本書，完整一條龍提供最正確的英語說法。

 # 作者序

　　明明學了好多年的英文，遇到國外客戶卻又不知道怎麼用嗎？

　　想了半天而說出口的英文卻是錯誤百出。OH ~ NO!!!

　　英文非我們母語，而台灣的英文教學又偏重中式教法。所以我們常常脫口而出的是中式英文而不自知。您知道我們常說的 double confirm, old people 其實是錯的嗎？其實稍稍換過來，就能說口好英語，本書沒有複雜的文法，只要簡單解釋給您聽，一定能學會！！

　　還有最道地又實用的商業英語，包含會議英文，文件英文，從接待國外客戶時正式說法到同事之間相處，聊天的口語表達，統統在這裡。並列舉我們常常犯的英文錯誤，告訴您，應該怎麼說更聰明！

商業英文意見交流 jessi.su@gmail.com

Jessica Su

目 次

Part I

會議篇
Meetings

Unit 1 廣告討論

Dialogue

Ivan	The first season sales result is quite disappointing. The performance of bottom line is not satisfactory at all .We must do better in the future!! I hope we can come to some creative ideas today.	第一季的銷售結果實在讓人失望，結果讓人一點也不滿意。我們必須有更好的表現。我希望今天能有些創意的想法。
Seven	Our team has taken different measures to diversify the product line. However, those steps haven't been sufficient; I think we need to expand our customer base.	我們團隊在產品線多元化上，採取了各種方法。但是成效不彰。我們需要擴展我們的客戶群。
Jack	I agree with Seven on that. However, it's not easy. As you know, there's a fierce competition in the digital component market.	我同意 Seven 的說法。但是，這可不容易。我們都知道電子配件市場十分競爭。

☹ Perhaps we should look at the idea of getting a star advertisement. It will be costly, I know, but it can associate our brand with the pubic. People will notice our brand. I'm sure this can catch people's eye.

或許我們可以考慮找明星廣告。我知道所費不貲，但是能將我們的品牌跟大眾連接起來。人們會注意我們的品牌，我相信這能吸引人們的目光。

Seven

Well, Jack, I have to say, that's a bold idea. Considering the extra expense, we have to make sure it works. The Vice president has made it very clear that if we mess this up, heads will roll! And ☹ the final date is in July.

Jack, 我必須説，這真是一個大膽的主意。考慮到這額外的高額花費，我們不能失敗。副總説過，如果我們把事情搞砸了，大家就倒楣了。而且我們的限期是在 7 月。

Jack

Thank you, Seven. I'm very aware of that! I've been researching this strategy and tactics closely for the past weeks. I know we haven't done it before. But the study shows it can attract a large amount of customers. Otherwise, our earphone won't get noticed among those competitions.

謝謝你，Seven。這我知道。我仔細研究這個策略好幾個星期了。我知道我們公司從來沒有先例過。但是，研究指出，名人廣告能吸引大量的顧客。否則，在眾多的競爭者之中，我們如何脱穎而出？

Ivan	An interesting thought, Jack. It's worth considering; do you have anyone on the list and the cost estimation?	很有意思的想法，Jack。這值得考慮。你手上有名單跟成本估算嗎？
Jack	Yes, here you are. As you can see from the file, Robert is the best choice. Teenagers love him, and Robert's movie was a hit in 2014. It's costly but worthwhile, trust me. Our earphone definitely can get quite a bit of exposure.	有的，在這裡。從檔案裡，你可以發現 Robert 是最好的人選。青少年喜歡他，而且在 2014 年，Robert 的電影十分賣座。雇請他代價高，但是值得。相信我，我們的耳機絕對能夠受到矚目的。
Ivan	Your research is quite persuasive. I'm impressed. It's a totally new idea. But I would say we should go for it.	你的研究很有說服力。不錯！這是一個全新的想法，但是我覺得我們應該試一試。

抓「龍」TIME

☹ Perhaps we should look at the idea of getting a star advertisement.

☺ Perhaps we should look at the idea of getting a celebrity endorsement.

☹ The final date is July.

☺ The deadline is July.

經典好用句

☺ **go for it** 大膽嘗試，努力爭取

If you really want the job, go for it.
如果你真喜歡那工作，努力去爭取吧。

☺ **mess up** 搞砸某事

If Adam messed up this project, he would probably be fired.
如果 Adam 搞砸這專案，他可能會被開除。

字彙精選

■ **satisfactory** *adj* 令人滿意的

Bally had gotten a satisfactory answer from Meredith
Bally 從 Meredith 那裡得到一個令人滿意的回覆。

■ **diversify** *v* 多元化

American culture has been diversified by the arrival of immigrants.
因為移民的到來，美國文化變的多元化了。

■ **sufficient** *adj* 足夠的

Alex didn't show up today, and his reason was not sufficient to justify his absence.
Alex 今天沒來，而且他的理由不足以證明他的缺席是有理的。

■ **associate** *v* 關聯，參加

Jim got caught yesterday because he was associated with a violent protest last month.
因為上個月參與暴力抗爭，Jim 昨日被捕。

■ **worthwhile** *adj* 值得的

Don't jump to conclusion; it's worthwhile to re-consider your decision.

不要妄下定論，你最好在重新考慮你的決定。

■ **definitely** *adv* 一定的，肯定的

About the air pollution, we should definitely do something to stop it.

針對空氣汙染，我們一定得採取行動。

抓龍術大公開

1. Perhaps we should look at the idea of getting a ~~star advertisement~~ celebrity endorsement.

或許我們可以考慮找明星廣告。

明星代言
☹star advertisement
☺celebrity endorsement

一般在說由明星代言某商品時，不用廣告 advertisement 這詞，而會使用 endorsement，以表示對於該產品或是公司的認可、背書之意。在英文中，一般會以 celebrity 來泛指所有的名人，而商品代言並不侷限僅由演藝人員代言，有可能是知名運動選手、名媛等，所以會以 celebrity endorsement 來稱由明星做廣告、或是名人代言。

celebrity n. 名人
endorsement n. 背書、贊同

例句

It's costly to have celebrity endorsement on the new product.

請明星來代言產品花費高昂。

2. The ~~final date~~ deadline is in July.

最後期限是在七月。

deadline 本為交稿的最後期限，後來統稱意指為各項事務的最後期限。
final date 指的是最後的日期，在語意上比較模糊，故以 deadline 來形容最後的期限較為恰當。

例句

The deadline for my new book is April 30.

我的新書最後截稿日是 4 月 30 日。

Unit 2 廣告討論-2

Dialogue

| Ivan | Jack, can you <u>bring us up to speed on</u> the result of the latest ad activity? The Robert one? | Jack, 可以跟我們説説最新的廣告的結果嗎?就 是 Robert 那 個 廣告。 |

| Jack | Sure, Ivan, my pleasure. I'm happy to report that the results of the initiative were better than we expected. The sales figures reveal an upward trend throughout the ad activity. In total, our sales scale has increased by 27 percent compared with the same period last year. | 當然,Ivan,這是我的榮幸。很高興的跟大家説明這主動的出擊效果比我們的預期還要好許多。透過廣告,各項銷售指標都顯示向上。總結的説,我們的銷售規模跟去年同期比較起來高出了 27%。 |

Ivan	That's good news indeed. Especially considering the competition in the digital component market is tough. Good job! Keep going. Seven, how does our new earphone product do as a result in the trade show, any plan?	的確，這真的是好消息。特別是考慮到數位配件市場的競爭十分激烈。做得好！！繼續保持這樣。Seven，我們的新耳機在資訊展的狀況如何？有什麼好計畫嗎？
Seven	We need more time to work out the details. After all, haste makes waste. But, so far, we have come up with some ideas; first, we can have some giving away prizes to attract people on the trade show.	我們需要時間把細節展開，畢竟欲速則不達。但是，目前我們有想到幾個點子，首先，我們打算在資訊展送些獎品來吸引人群。
Ivan	Seven suggests giving away prizes to people attending the trade show. Honestly speaking, I'm kind of like this idea, too. Are there any other suggestions, Seven?	Seven 建議在資訊展上送獎品。老實說，我還滿喜歡這主意的。還有其他想法嗎？Seven？

Seven	How about hiring some show girls dancing on a stage near our booth that will definitely catch people's eye?	如果説我們雇請一些秀展女孩在我們攤位旁的舞台跳舞，這樣一定會大受注目的。
Jack	I'm not sure that would work for our products. Also, it would be quite an expense. Most importantly, the bottom line is that it's not budgeted for.	我不確定我們的產品可以這樣行銷。這項花費太高，重點是，我們沒有此預算。
Ivan	Well, we appreciate the bold suggestion, Seven. But I agree with Jack. For the other thing, we don't have much time to put the show girls together and train them well. If we make much our effort on something we don't familiar with, then we aren't focus on our products. Perhaps we can serve some free drink.	嗯，Seven，你這建議很大膽吶。但是我同意Jack。另外一點是，我們沒時間去找這些秀展女孩，然後好好訓練她們。如果我們花太多時間在我們不熟悉的活動上，我們將無法全力投入我們產品。或許我們可以提供免費飲料。

Jack	Free drinking is an excellent suggestion. People love free stuff. I prefer free drink than show girl. How about you? Steven.	免費飲料是個很棒的點子，人們對免費的東西總是難以抗拒。跟秀展女孩比起來，我傾向於免費飲料。Seven，你呢？
Seven	That sounds great!	聽起來不錯！

抓「龍」TIME

☹ prefer free drink than show girl.
☺ prefer free drink to show girl.

經典好用句

☺ **bring… up to speed on…**　提供某人關於某事的消息
Jack is going to bring us up to speed on the latest promotion.
Jack 將會告訴我們促銷的最新訊息。

☺ **Haste makes waste.**　欲速則不達
Haste makes waste. I hope you had learned the lesson.
欲速則不達，我希望你學到教訓了。

字彙精選

■ **initiative** *adj* 初步的; *n* 主動的行動

We must take the initiative to win the market share.
我們必須採取主動才能贏得市場佔有率。

■ **reveal** *v* 顯示

Janet has refused to reveal the person who took them to the military base.
Janet 拒絕透露是誰帶她們去軍事基地的。

■ **compare with** 與之相比

Compare with other countries, Taiwan Health insurance is quite advanced.
與其他國家相比,台灣的健康保險相對先進。

■ **tough** *adj/adv* 頑強的,困難的

She is tough and ambitious, and will be the candidate for the 2016 president election.
她很堅強又野心勃勃,是未來 2016 年的總統候選人。

■ **budget** *v/n* 預算

The cosmetic company has budgeted $ 20 million for advertising. They hire a superstar as their product endorser.
化妝品公司編了 2 千萬的廣告預算。他們僱請超級明星作產品代言人。

■ **make effort** 努力

All of us make an extra effort to achieve the annual sales goal.
為了達成年度銷售目標,我們全部都格外努力

Webber	You what? What is your mean? Are you saying that you are leaving? Mark, I wasn't even aware that you'd been scouting around. Is it something I've done or haven't done? May I know why?	你什麼？你的意思指說你要離開了嗎？Mark，我怎麼都不知道你在找工作。是我哪裡做得不夠好？你為什麼要離職呢？
Mark	Webber, it's not about you. You've been really nice to me, and I'm grateful that you taught me so much.	Webber，我離職的原因不是因為你。你對我一直很好，也對我指導許多。
Webber	Then, tell me the reason if you are convenient. Is this about Peter?	那麼，如果你方便的話，告訴我原因吧，是因為 Peter 嗎？
Mark	No~ I have to make it clear that Peter is not correlated with my decision although we were competitors. I've learned a lot from him and appreciate the opportunity I've been given here.	不不。我必須澄清我的決定跟 Peter 無關，雖然我們一直是競爭關係。但是我從他身上獲益匪淺。我也很感謝公司給我的機會。
Webber	I must say that I'm confused. If there's nothing wrong, why are you leaving?	我必須說我越聽越糊塗了，如果一切都好，那你為什麼要離職？

Mark	Well, I feel I've grown professionally as much as I can here and really need some new challenges. To be honest, I've got a great position in the new company, and the pay is too good to turn down.	是這樣的，我覺得我在 Grey 公司學的專業學知識已經到了極限，我需要新的挑戰跟刺激。老實說，新公司給我很棒的職位及無法拒絕的薪資。
Webber	I see. Mark, you know how much I value your work there. If you came to me earlier, we might have had a chance to make a better offer.	我了解。你知道我很看重你在這裡的工作。如果你早點來找我，我們或許還有機會可以談談更好的條件。
Mark	I'm sorry, Webber.	我很抱歉，Webber。
Webber	I suppose that it's too late to make the counteroffer?	我猜現在再跟你重談待遇也沒辦法了吧。
Mark	I'm afraid so. I had made the decision, it's a chance of the lifetime and I should take it.	恐怕如此，我已經做了決定，這是難得一遇的好機會，應該要把握。
Webber	Ok, Mark, I respect your decision; wish you the best in your new career.	好的。Mark，我尊重你的決定。希望你在職場上一帆風順。

| Mark | Thanks for your understanding and support that really means a lot to me. I won't leave right away; this is my two weeks' notice. | 謝謝你的諒解跟支持，這對我很重要。我還不會馬上離職，我還會再待兩星期。 |

抓「龍」TIME

☹ What is your mean?
☺ What do you mean?
☹ Tell me the reason if you are convenient.
☺ Tell me the reason if it is convenient for you.

經典好用句

☺ **to make a long story short**　長話短說

A: Hey , do you know what happened to Vincent?
B: I have no clue, but please make a long story short, I don't have whole day.
A: Well, he got fired last week.
A：嘿，你知道 Vincent 怎麼了嗎？
B：沒點頭緒，不過請長話短說，我沒時間。
A：這個嘛～他上週被辭退了。

☺ **it's not about you**　與你無關

= This has nothing to do with you.

A: I felt sorry for Melinda, she got a big fight with her husband.

B: Don't worry, it's not about you.

A：我對 Melinda 感到很抱歉，她跟他先生大吵一架。

B：別擔心，那與你無關 .

字彙精選

■ **scout** *v* 查探，物色

My friends are visiting; I've been scouting around the town for a better restaurant.

我朋友即將來訪，我到處在市裡找好餐廳。

■ **turn down** 拒絕；調小

Michael just turned down Vincent's suggestion; they won't have a Christmas dinner together.

Michael 剛拒絕 Vincent 的提議，他們聖誕節不會一塊吃晚餐。

Please turn down the music; I'm studying for the test.

請將音樂調小聲，我正在為考試準備。

■ **value** *v* 重視

His professional opinion is highly valued by the Sales manager.

業務經理很看重他的專業意見。

■ **suppose** *v* 猜測，認為，應該

They were supposed to arrive the hotel 2 hours ago;
however, their plane was delayed.

他們應該 2 個小時前就抵達飯店了，但是他們的飛機延誤了。

■ **I'm afraid so.** 恐怕如此

A: Are you saying that Kelly was kicked out of school?
B: I'm afraid so.

A：你是說 Kelly 被學校踢出來了。
B：恐怕如此。

■ **notice** *n/v* 通知，注意

Owen's special talents attracted teacher's notice.

Owen 特殊的才能引起老師的注意。

抓龍術大公開

1. ~~What is your mean?~~ What do you mean?
   你是什麼意思呢？

   此錯誤用法為由中文句直接翻譯成英文的用法，**mean** 在英文當中的詞性分別可做動詞、名詞及形容詞使用。當名詞使用時，**mean** 做「中間」、「平均值」解釋，做為形容詞時則有「刻薄的」、「吝嗇」的意思，在此句中，**mean** 應當做動詞使用，雖然以 mean ＋ ing，使其成為名詞可做「意思」解釋，而"**What is your meaning?**"在文法上也無誤，但最好還是在這裡將 mean 做動詞使用，"**What do you mean?**"才是道地的說法。

   例句
   > A: What do you mean? You mean you can't work with Penney any more.
   > B: Yep, she is so annoying.
   > A：你指的是什麼？你是説你再也沒辦法跟 Penny 一起工作？
   > B：對，她好煩人。

2. Tell me the reason, if ~~you are convenient~~ it's convenient for you.
   如果你方便的話，告訴我理由。

如果你方便的話

☹If you are convenient.

☺If it's convenience for you.

convenient 無法直接形容人，convenient 一般是用來形容事物，用以詢問人是否方便的時候，應加上虛構主詞 it，成為"Is it convenient for you?"才是正確的說法。

例句

I like to visit you this summer, if it's convenience for you.

如果方便的話，這個夏天我想去拜訪你們。

Unit 4 換供應商

Dialogue

Webber	We all know about the problems that we've been dealing with Pollo. Their sales representatives always <u>make empty promises</u> about the raw material delivery. That resulted in lots of trouble for our capacity planning.	大家都很清楚我們最近因為 Pollo 這公司面臨許多問題。Pollo 的業務總是答應我們原料會準時交貨,但又食言。這導致我們的生產計劃十分混亂。
Christian	I have to say, in my case, some shipments were delayed because of Pollo. They didn't deliver the raw material on time, so our products can't be finished as the plan. It really annoys me; I suggest that we should stop cooperating with Pollo.	我必須說,在我這邊,有些貨都因為 Pollo 而延後出貨了,他們沒有準時將原料送達,造成產品無法依計畫完成。我覺得很煩人,是時候要終止與 Pollo 的合作了。

Meredith	I'm not sure. There seem to be a few different opinions regarding this subject. Some people feel we should give Pollo another chance. Because ☹they so supply raw material with the most competitive price, then we can reduce our cost. Should we put the decision to a vote?	這點我不是很確定。關於這點，似乎有些不同看法。有些人覺得我們應該給 Pollo 一次機會。因為 Pollo 的確提供給我們最優惠的價格，有助於我們成本降低。我們是不是來投票決定好了？
Webber	Sure, I hope that we can reach an agreement today. I think it's a crunch time for our sales project. Is everyone in favor of ending the contract with Pollo and finding another supplier? It looks like most people are in favor of the contract termination.	當然，這事關緊要，我希望我們今天能有個結論。是不是大家都贊成中止與 Pollo 的合約，然後另尋供應商？看起來大家都贊成這合約應該中止。
Christian	Now, we have to look for a new supplier. Last year, when we attended the Medical Supply show in Seattle, there were many new suppliers, ☹do you remind anyone, Webber?	那現在，我們要考慮的是新供應商。去年，我們參加西雅圖醫療供應展時，很許多供應商碰面。Webber，你有記得誰嗎？

Webber	If my memory serves me right, I've spoken with the VP of Northwind. He seems to be a very reliable businessman. Their price may not be the best, but their service and product quality were very impressive.	如果我沒記錯的話，我曾和 Northwind 的副總聊過，他似乎是個可靠的商人。他們的價格不是最低的，但是服務跟品質令人印象深刻。
Christian	I remember him, Mr. Glen. We had a long conversation in the show. Glen is very professional on the raw material; I guess he has been in this business over 20 years. But, we didn't sign the contract with Northwind, their price was 7% higher than Pollo.	我記得他，Glen 先生，我們在會場上聊了一陣子。Glen 在原物料上十分的專業，我想他好像做這行超過 20 年了。但是最後，因為他們的價格比 Pollo 高出 7%，我們沒有和 Northwind 簽約。
Webber	Well, besides the cost, we should consider the supplier credibility as well. Meredith, set a meeting with Northwind's Mr. Glen next week.	嗯，除了成本。我們應該將供應商的誠信也考慮進去。Meredith，安排一下跟 Northwind 的 Glen 先生下週會議。
Meredith	I'm right on it.	我這就去辦。

抓「龍」TIME

☹ They so supply raw material with the most competitive price.
☺ They do supply raw material with the most competitive price.
☹ Do you remind anyone?
☺ Do you remember anyone?

經典好用句

☺ **make empty promises**　食言，說空話

Russell keeps making empty promises to his children; they refuse to talk with him anymore.

Russell 總是對他的孩子食言，所以他們拒絕跟他說話。

☺ **it's a crunch time**　這是一個關鍵時刻

Maggie got USD5,000 loan from the bank, it's a crunch time for her family business.

Maggie 從銀行貸款了 USD$5,000，這是她家族事業的關鍵時刻。

字彙精選

■ **capacity planning**　產能計畫

Capacity planning is very complicated for the manufacturing system.

對生產系統來說，產能計畫是很複雜的。

■ **agreement** *n* 意見一致，合同

I'm glad that we finally have reached an agreement on the loan contract.

我很高興我們在貸款合約上意見一致。

■ **in favor of** 贊成

All employees are all in favor of the spring vacation; it's time to take a break.

所有員工都贊成春假假期，是該好好休息。

■ **termination** *n* 中止，結束

The government expects that the dispute can be a satisfactory termination.

政府期待抗爭能夠有個滿意的結束。

■ **besides** *adv* 除此之外

The SUV is too expensive; besides, our garage is too small for the SUV.

那台 SUV 太貴了，此外我們的車庫太小根本不能停 SUV 車。

■ **credibility** *n* 可靠，可信

The credibility of the military has been seriously impaired by the recently scandal.

近來的醜聞讓軍方的信譽重挫。

抓龍術大公開

1. They ~~so~~ do supply raw material with the most competitive price

在原物料上，他們的確提供最好的價格。

在英文中，要強調一個句子時，口語中可以用重讀表示要強調的地方。說寫上可以將要強調的部分擺在句首；或是以特定的形容詞或是副詞來強調。so 應該用來強調形容詞及副詞，不能用於強調動詞上。但有特例，如：I so want to go to the summer camp.（我非常想去夏令營。）這樣的用法被稱作是青少年俚語，不適用於職場及正式場合中。而這裡介紹的是以助動詞 do+ 動詞原形的方式來強調語氣。這一句如果要以副詞強調的話，可以寫 really，有"very, very much"的意思。

2. Do you ~~remind~~ remember anyone?
你有記得誰嗎？

記得
☹remind
☺remember

在英文中有好幾種與「記憶」有關的字彙，例如這裡提到的 remind 及 remember，另外還有像是 recall，recollect 及 reminisce，這幾種的記憶方式都不太相同。在句中的 remind 應做為「想起」，為有相似的兩件事物，或是某某東西使我想到什麼，也可做「提醒」解釋。例如：

> Those photos remind me of my childhood in China.
> （這些照片讓我想起童年在中國的日子。）
> 而這一句是要問某人是否記得，則應該用 remember，由記憶中浮現出的印象，做「想起」、「記得」解釋。

例句
> I remember that Jimmy always made stupid jokes.
> 我記得 Jimmy 總愛講些無聊的笑話。

Unit 5 會前準備

Meredith and Webber are in the conference room.
Meredith 跟 Webber 在會議室

Webber	Meredith, is everything going well for tomorrow's meeting with Mr. Jackson? I don't want any erratic factor happen. You know such an important client could easily be lost thorough a silly mistake. Besides, I heard that Jackson is easy to become angry.	Meredith，明天跟 Jackson 開會的事項都準備好了嗎？我不想冒任何的險。你知道我們可能因為一個小失誤而失去重要的客戶。除此之外，我聽說 Jackson 是個易怒的人。
Meredith	You are so right. But don't worry, everything is under control. Everyone in the office and factory management has been told by special notice 1 week ago. I've also confirmed with a meeting schedule with Wilson, he has to do the presentation for Mr. Jackson.	您說對了。但是不要擔心。事情都在掌控之中。辦公室的每個人及工廠的管理階層，早在一星期前就收到特別通知了。我也跟 Wilson 確認好會議行程。他會為 Jackson 先生做簡報。

Webber	Well then, we should set the meeting schedule once and for all.	那好，報告會議行程是怎麼安排的？
Meredith	Sure. At the beginning, I'll briefly introduce you and me. After that, Wilson will make a full presentation about our company. And I'd like to set up a factory tour after the meeting. Then Mr. Jackson shall the whole picture about our company and be convince of the mutual cooperation.	是的，開始時，我會簡短的介紹您跟我。之後，Wilson 針對我們公司做一個完整的簡報介紹。會議後，我安排了去工廠參觀。這樣 Jackson 對我們公司就能有更多的了解，進而對雙方的互助合作更具信心。
Webber	Sounds good. Remember, Mr. Jackson is as sharp as a tack, so we need to pay extra attention on detail. How about the samples? Did you get samples ready?	聽起來不錯。記住，Jackson 很精明的，細節上我們得多留意。樣品呢？你準備好了嗎？
Meredith	Yes, they are in the conference room.	準備好了，都在會議室裡。
Webber	You'd better be, and re-check on all the details.	最好如此，細節要再三確認。

Meredith	I'll get right on it, actually, I'll spend the rest of my day proofreading all the supporting documentation.	會的。事實上，今天我要看完所有的準備資料。
Webber	Have you come up with anything about the sole agent contract?	獨家代理權合約的事，你想清楚了嗎？
Meredith	Yes, I presume that Mr. Jackson will emphasize the discount rate and commission. I'm not sure if I have full authorization on the negotiation.	是的，我推測 Jackson 先生會著重在折扣率跟佣金上。但是，關於這兩項，我不確定我是否有得到公司的充分談判授權。
Webber	Of course you have. As I had explained to you, we are a team. Your decision will be fully supportive. And I believe that you will make the right decision for our company's best interest.	當然，你有決定權。像我之前跟你解釋過的，我們是一個團隊。公司對你的決定會完全支持，而且我相信你會為了公司最佳利益而做出最好的決定。
Meredith	Thank you, Webber. I'll do my best.	謝謝你，Webber。我會盡力的。

抓「龍」TIME

☹ Jackson is easy to become angry.
☺ Jackson becomes angry easily.
☹ I had explained to you.
☺ I had explained it to you.

經典好用句

☺ **everything is under control**　一切都在控制之中

The typhoon is coming, stay in your house until everything is under control

颱風來了，留在家裡，直到一切受到控制為止。

☺ **Have you come up with anything?**　你有想到什麼好方法嗎？

We need to improve our QC style, have you come up with anything?

我們的品管系統需要改進，你有想到什麼好方法嗎？

字彙精選

■ **erratic**　*adj*　不穩定的

The erratic economic policy makes people suffering from inflation.

不穩定的經濟政策導致人民遭受通貨膨脹之苦。

■**documentation** *n* 文件，參考資料

Without proper documentation, you can't go to any country.

沒有相關的證件，你那個國家都不能去。

■**whole picture** 全局，全貌

Rick would look at the whole pictures before making a big decision.

在做任何重大決定之前，Rick 都會先考慮大局。

■**emphasize** *v* 強調，著重

For a better environment, the reporter emphasized the importance of alternative energy.

為了更好的環境，記者不斷強調替代能源的重要性。

■**authorization** *n* 授權

Without government authorization, nobody can enter the security area.

沒有政府的許可，沒有人能進入禁區。

■**supportive** *adj* 支持的

About Rick's new escape plan, Glen is very supportive.

關於 Rick 新的逃脫計畫，Glen 十分的支持。

抓龍術大公開

1. Jackson ~~is easy to become angry~~ becomes angry easily.

Jackson很容易生氣

容易生氣
☹easy to become angry
☺become angry easily

正確説法除了上句之外，還可以説"Jackson easily becomes angry."副詞 easily 可置於動詞 become 的前面或是後面做修飾。

例句

Shawn has bad temper, he becomes angry easily. You should be more carefully.
Shawn 脾氣很壞，他很容易生氣。你要留意。

2. As I had explained it to you.
像我之前跟你解釋過的。

我之前向你解釋過的。
☹I had explained to you.
☺I had explained it to you.

explain 的用法有兩種，如下：
a. explain sth to sb （最常用）
b. explain to sb sth
正確説法中的 it 為虛主詞，代表 sth，但如果要用 b 用法，則需要加入下一句"we are a team"，以 that 子句的方式表示 sth，可寫成"As I had explained to you that we are a team."。

例句

I had explained it to you. The picnic was cancelled because of the bad weather.
我已經跟你解釋過了，因為天氣不好，野餐取消了。

Unit 6　客戶來訪

Dialogue

| Meredith | Welcome, good afternoon, it's a pleasure to finally meet you in person. I'm Meredith, the new Sales representative. I hope that both of you had a pleasant flight. | 歡迎，午安。很高興終於見到您本人，我是 Meredith，Grey 產品的新業務代表。希望您一路過來飛行還愉快。 |

Please take a seat. As you know, Grey Products intends to expand into Western Canada and the US market. We need a well-known distributor to achieve this goal together. To be honest, it would be a great start if we could secure a deal with a respectful distributor like you.

請坐。如您所知，我們公司正打算擴展加拿大西岸及美國市場。我們需要一位名聲響亮的經銷商來一起完成這任務。老實說，我們很榮幸能跟貴公司這麼信譽良好的公司合作。

Jackson	Thank you, Meredith. <u>The pleasure is mine.</u> Actually, we have heard about Grey Products long time ago. It's very famous in medical equipment industry. We truly hope that with Grey equipment, our patient can have more proper care in the hospital.	謝謝你，Meredith。我們覺得很榮幸來拜訪貴公司。事實上，Grey 產品在市場上聞名已久，是相當有名氣的醫療器材公司。我們希望藉由 Grey 產品，我們能為醫院的病人提供更完善的照顧。
Meredith	Thank you, Jackson. I'll be responsible for the first round of negotiation there. I hope we can make some significant achievement during your stay in Taiwan, At the same movement, my supervisor, Mr. Webber will join us.	我將負責第一輪的協商。希望在您停留台北的期間我們的協商能有顯著的成果。同時，我的主管，Webber 先生也會加入我們的協商。

Jackson	I know your company wants to expand the market into Western Canada and United States. All you need is a good channel of distribution, through our effective distribution work, you will get a head start on other competitors. Without a doubt, I'd like to secure a deal with a respectful and well-known manufacture like you as well.	我知道貴公司正在尋找加拿大西岸及美國地區的經銷商，以拓展當地市場。您需要的是一個好的銷售管道。透過我們高效率的經銷努力，貴公司將會在其他競爭者中脫穎而出，取得領先。毫無疑問的，本公司跟榮幸能跟像貴公司一樣知名，信譽良好的製造商合作。
Webber	Welcome, I'm Webber. I think the future of our cooperation is good. We can start from going thought our products line. There are some catalogues in front of your desk. These are the full information of our products. In addition, we have arranged you visiting our factory this afternoon. By visiting our factory, we hope that you can understand how we manufacture those products, and the S.O.P. of quality inspection.	歡迎您，我是Webber。我相信我們的合作前景可期，我們可以先看過我們的產品開始。各位桌上有目錄，這些是我公司產品的所有資料。還有，我們已經安排好您下午參觀我們工廠的行程。我們希望藉由參觀我們工廠，您可了解商品是如何生產出來的，及我們對品質檢驗的標準流程。

| Jackson | Thank you, Webber. <u>That's very thoughtful.</u> In fact, that's the main reason of our trip. They said "Seeing is believing". | 謝 謝 您，Webber。這實在太貼心了。事實上，我們此次前來的目的即為此。我們想參觀工廠。俗話說"眼見為憑"。 |

抓「龍」TIME

☹ I think the future of our cooperation is good.

☺ I think the future of our cooperation is promising.

經典好用句

☺ **The pleasure is mine.** 我的榮幸

在商業場合當中，初見對方，總要客套兩句。最常使用的是"It's my pleasure to meet with you."（很高興見到您。）。

這時，我們可以回對方"The pleasure is mine."，意思是，您太客氣了，這是我的榮幸。

☺ **That's very thoughtful.** 太體貼了

We received the flower, that's very thoughtful of you.

我們收到花了，你實在太體貼了。

字彙精選

■**in person** 本人

After 2 years email communication, Katharina finally met her client in person.

經過兩年多的電子郵件往來，**Katharina** 終於見到她客戶本人了。

■**distributor** *n* 經銷商

There are many Sony distributors in Japan

Sony 公司在日本有很多經銷商。

■**respectful** *adj* 令人尊敬的

Miss Chen is a very respectful lady; she has denoted lots of money to school.

陳小姐是令人尊敬的女性，她捐了許多錢給學校。

■**catalogue** *n.* 目錄

Please provide all your catalogues; we are very interested in your products.

請提供所有的目錄，因為我們對貴公司的產品很感興趣。

■**medical equipment** 醫療設備

Apex is a famous medical equipment manufacture in Taiwan.

Apex 是台灣有名的醫療設備製造商。

■**S.O.P.** 標準流程，常聽到的**SOP**
= **Standard Operation Procedure**

To work more efficiently, we need to improve the S.O.P. of the meeting.

為了工作更有效率，我們必須改善會議的標準流程。

抓龍術大公開

1. I think the future of our cooperation is ~~good~~ promising.

我覺得我們合作的未來會很好。

這一句話本身沒有問題，文法也正確，但用在職場，即與客戶會面時所談，則過於平淡，說服力也稍顯薄弱，所以建議以 **promising** 來代替 **good**，讓整句話聽起來為更有願景，有前景可期的感覺。

promising   adj   充滿希望的

例句

Due to his hard working, Jack is the promising star in his company.

因為辛勤工作，Jack 成為公司明日之星。

Unit 7　佣金

Dialogue

Jackson	Very impressive. The facilities in your factory are quite advanced. I'm surprised that Taiwan manufacturer has the world-leading technology in the medical equipment industry. Generally speaking, I considered Japan and Canada are the pioneers in this field. But, after my Taiwan trip, I won't say that again.

實在讓人印象深刻呀，你們工廠的設備相當先進。我很訝異台灣醫療設備產業製造商，擁有領先世界的技術。一般來說，我總認為日本跟加拿大才是這產業的領先者。不過，經過我這趟台灣之旅，我不會再這樣想了。

Meredith	Thank you. Actually, we spend lots manpower and resources on research and new technology development every year. The annual budget is quite high. Because Webber believes that the innovation is the key to the future. It's not easy at the beginning; however, after many years, we already surpass other competitors.	謝謝您的稱讚。事實上，我們每年花費許多人力物力在研究開發上。年度預算是很高的，因為 Webber 相信，唯有創新才能開創未來。一開始並不容易，過了這些年，我們已經超越其他競爭者了。
Jackson	Now, I'm more confident of our cooperation. Let's get back to the business. If our company acts as Grey Products sole agent in Western Canada and the United States, we think that we should be rewarded for volume sales.	對於我們的合作我越來越有信心了。該是談生意的時候了。如果我們公司成為 Grey's 產品的加拿大西岸跟美國的獨家代理商，大量的銷售額是否有折扣呢？
Meredith	That sounds reasonable; since you are the biggest distributor in North America. Can you give me the exact number?	當然，既然貴公司是北美地區最大的供應商，這聽來很合理。不過你可以給我具體的數字嗎？

Jackson	We think 7% discount on orders over US$100,000 per month is acceptable, and a commission of 15% on net-list prices.	我認為每個月超過 10 萬美元的訂單,必須有 7% 的折扣。而且我們的佣金為淨價的 15%。
Meredith	We can accept the 7% discount, if your company is able to sell such a large volume. But the 15% commission? I don't think I have the delegation of authority to make this decision. I'll have Webber to review this issue.	Meredith:如果你的銷售額可以達到 10 萬美金的話,7% 折扣我們可以接受。但是佣金 15%?這項決定超過我的職權了,我請 Webber 來重新審視這項議題。
Webber	Jackson, I think we can accept 10% commission on the net-price. Can we agree to payment once a month?	Jackson,我想我們只能接受 10% 佣金。你們能每個月支付貨款嗎?
Jackson	OK, I'll take 10% commission. But we prefer to make the payment per quarter; we are more conservative on cash-flow.	好,那就 10% 佣金。每季付款對我們比較適合,因為我們的現金流很保守。
Webber	Okay, if you insist.	好吧,如果你堅持的話。

Jackson	What's the contract duration? I hope it can be started from next month, and finish on July 2017. It will be 2 years.	合約期多久？我希望能從下個月開始，到 2017 年 7 月結束。2 年。
Meredith	We can accept the 2 years contract duration.	2 年約我們接受。
Jackson	I like to sign this sole agent contract asap. Strike while the iron is hot.	我想要把這獨家代理合約盡快簽下，打鐵要趁熱呀。

抓「龍」TIME

☹ Can you give me the exact number?

☺ Can you give me the concrete number?

☹ I hope it can be started from next month, and finish on July 2017.

☺ I hope it can be started from next month, and expire on July 2017.

經典好用句

☺ **if you insist**　如果你堅持要的話

通常表示不是很認同對方的話，但是若對方要求，也是會盡力配合。

A: I like to invite Patrick to my birthday party.

B: Ok, if you insist.

A：我想邀請 Patrick 來我的生日派對。

B：好吧，如果你堅持的話。

☺ **Strike while the iron is hot.**　打鐵趁熱

A: I think Melinda may take our counteroffer; she is very satisfied with our samples

B: Great, you should strike while the iron is hot.

A：我想 Melinda 應該會接受我們的還價，她對我們的樣品很滿意。

B：太好了，你應該要打鐵趁熱。

字彙精選

■ **advanced** *adj* 先進的

Without advanced technical skills, Grey products can't get the order.

若沒有先進的技術，Grey 產品不可能贏得此張訂單。

■ **surpass** *v* 超越

Jack gave an excellent presentation that surpassed everyone's expectation.

Jack 絕佳的簡報超過大家的預期。

■ **reward** *v* 酬謝，獎賞

He was rewarded with a trip to Paris.

他得到巴黎之旅的獎勵。

■ **delegation** *n* 授權，代表團

During the conference, the French delegation was carrying a message of thanks to President Obama.

在會議期間，法國代表團向歐巴馬總統轉達謝意。

■ **authority** *n* 權力，當局

You have no authority asking me to leave, this is public space.

你沒有權力叫我離開，這裡是公開場所。

■ **prefer to** 寧願，更喜歡

A: What's your summer vacation plan?

B: We don't know yet, but we prefer to go to Denmark.

A：暑假要怎麼安排。

B：我們還不確定，但是我們比較想去丹麥。

抓龍術大公開

1. Can you give me the ~~exact~~ concrete number?
可以給我一個具體的數字嗎？

具體的數字
☹exact number
☺concrete number

exact number 指的是確切的數字，通常會是需要相當精準的數字，但在對話中，因為還在預估階段，所以應該使用 concrete number，請對方以已知狀況預估一個數字，以利評估佣金的部分。另外在這樣的對話中，也可以用 ballpark number（大概的數字）來代替 concrete number。
concrete　n/adj　水泥；具體的、確實的

例句

He has no concrete evidence to prove that Katherine was the thief.
他沒有確實的證據能證明 Katherine 是小偷。

2. I hope it can be started from next month, and ~~finish~~ expire on July 2017.
我希望能從下個月開始，到2017年7月結束。

合約結束
☹finish
☺expire

合約結束不使用"finish"這單字，正確用法應為 expire，指文件、合約、協議等的到期。

expiry date 有效期限

例句

This milk has passed its expiry date.

這牛奶已經過了到期日。

Unit 8 計畫參展

Dialogue

In the Meeting

Joseph To increase our turnover in 2015, we are going to expand our market into North America Market this year, and the main product will be our new luggage, the Star 1, with the latest design and technical material. It's the best item in our factory; I hope our sales representative can be more aggressive on promoting this new item.

為增加公司在 2015 年的營業額，今年，我們決定擴展北美市場，而主要的產品就是我們的新型行李箱－星辰一號，它有最新的設計跟科技材質。是我們工廠的明星產品，我希望我們的業務可以更積極的推廣這項產品。

Claire　Yes, I agree with the Joseph. According to the statistical data, at present the Star 1 has already got a 10% market share in Japan. It's really incredible achievement. I believe that Star 1 will be a good start for North America market。 However, on the other hand, my concern is the customers don't like the expensive price. They like cheap price. The cost of Star 1 is relatively high because of the high technology fabric.

是的，我同意 Joseph 說的。根據數據，目前星辰一號在日本市占率有 10%，這實在是項了不起的成就。開拓北美市場，星辰一號是個很好的開始。但是在另一方面，我擔心客戶不喜歡很昂貴的產品，客戶總被價格吸引。而星辰一號因為採用高科技布料而成本相對較高。

Cindy　Joseph, May I have a word, I suggest that we can attend a Travel Exhibition in the L.A. next month, it's the most famous luggage exhibition in the world. We can take this great opportunity introducing our new product to the world wild buyers. People will understand the Star 1 is not only a fashion luggage, but also an innovation, then focus on its function not its price.

Joseph，我可以發言嗎？我建議我們可以參加下個月在 LA 的旅行用品展覽，這是世界上最有名的行李箱展覽。我們可以借此難得機會介紹我們的新產品給買家認識。可以讓人們更了解我們的商品，星辰一號不光是時尚的行李箱，更是創新的發明。進而注意星辰一號的功能，而不是它的價格。

Joseph	Good point, I agree with you. Cindy, arrange the business trip to LA next month, and ship the star 1 to the exhibition in advance. David, you go to LA with us, you had experience on dealing with American customer. Let's focus on this project. I want to have a big success on the show.	説的好，我同意妳。Cindy，安排下個月去參展的事。先把我們的商品，星辰一號運送到展覽會場去。David，你跟我們去，你之前有做美國市場的經驗。我希望商品能在展覽上受到歡迎，大家一起把這事努力做好。
David	Sure, Joseph, I'm glad that my experience is helpful. I'll submit a brief American market report to you before this Friday. We can have some potential customer list and marketing strategies in advance.	沒問題，Joseph，我很高興我的經驗能幫上忙。這週五之前，我會交給您一份美國市場的簡短報告。我們可以預先整理出潛在客戶名單跟擬訂市場策略。

抓「龍」TIME

☹ The customers don't like the expensive price, they like cheap price.

☺ The customer can't accept the higher price, they prefer more competitive price.

經典好用句

☺ **on the other hand**　另一方面

The China economic has increased sharply; however on the other hand, the pollution is getting worse and worse.

中國經濟成場快速，然而，在另一方面，汙染也日趨嚴重。

☺ **take this great opportunity**　藉此難得的機會

Elaine likes to take this great opportunity introducing her fiancé to the family.

Elaine 想要藉此難得機會，將她未婚夫介紹給家人認識。

字彙精選

■ **latest**　*adj*　最新的

The latest movies "Kingsman The secret Service" is very popular.

最新電影金牌特務，很受歡迎。

■ **market share** 市占率

ABC company is fighting to retrieve its market share.
ABC 正為它的市場占有率而努力。

■ **incredible achievement** 不起的成就

For the recently year, Fetal surgery becomes possible and practical, it's an incredible achievement of human medical.
近年來，胎兒手術越來越切實可行。這是人類醫學上了不起的成就。

■ **potential** *adj* 有潛力的

Due to his high potential on Taekwondo, Owen's coach appointed him in next game.
Owen 在跆拳道上潛力無窮，他的教練指定他下局出賽。

■ **strategy** *n* 策略

I think we have to work out a strategy to deal with this situation.
我認為我們必須制訂策略來面對這個問題。

抓龍術大公開

1. The customers ~~don't like~~ can't accept the ~~expensive~~ higher price, they ~~like~~ prefer ~~cheap~~ more competitive price.
顧客不喜歡很貴的商品，他們喜歡便宜的。

不喜歡
☹don't like
☺can't accept

喜歡
☹like
☺prefer

較貴的價格
☹expensive price
☺higher price

便宜的價格
☹cheap price
☺more competitive price

口語裡的喜歡、不喜歡，我們常用 like, doesn't like 來表示。高價跟低價則用 cheap（便宜的）跟 expensive（昂貴的）這兩個形容詞。但是在商用英語裡，會採用比較婉轉的說法。用 can't accept 來代替 don't like，prefer 來代替 like；higher 來代替 expensive，more competitive 來代替 cheap。其中 cheap 這字，在商用英文中甚少使用。不論是供應商或是買方，說到價格時，多使用 competitive price（具競爭力價格）或是 good price（好的價格）。在中文中常說便宜，在英文中應避免使用 cheap 此字。

Unit 9 新市場

Dialogue

In the meeting
會議中

Joseph Now every one of you has looked over my proposal, perhaps we could briefly go over it again. One of our top selling products lines in Taiwan is the small size washer and dryer units, model ZZ-123 and YY-246 respectively. Due to their compact size and high efficiency, those two items sell very well. So, <u>my opinion is that</u> we can promote those 2 items to the States, I want to hear your views on this subject.

在座的各位都應該看過我的提案了，也許我們可以再簡短的瀏覽一次。我們 XYZ 公司產品，在台灣最暢銷的是小型洗衣機跟烘衣機。型號分別為 ZZ-123 跟 YY-246。因為這兩項產品，尺寸小，效率高，一直十分暢銷。我目前有個想法，我們或許可以將這兩樣產品推銷到美國市場去。各位怎麼想？

Cindy	Yes, you are right, ZZ-123 and YY-246 are our best-selling products. The outlook is very attractive and in style. But, I'm afraid that I cannot agree to your proposal. As far as I'm concerned, Americans prefer large household appliances. Our products ZZ-123 and YY-246 are not good for the States' market.	你說的沒錯，ZZ-123 跟 YY-246 是我們的暢銷產品。外型十分吸引人，時尚。但是，我恐怕不能同意你的提案。就我而言，美國市場偏向大型家電產品。我們的 ZZ-123 跟 YY-246 不適合美國市場。
Claire	Maybe Cindy is right, but it's just a stereotype for the States market. I have a different idea. We can tap into the States market with specialized needs, such as college students with small apartments, and single and elderly people who don't have to do a lot of laundry. And most important is that they don't have enough space for large household appliances. From my research, there is no other competitor in the small household appliance field in the States. This leads me to believe that there is a need which can be filled by our products.	Cindy 說的或許對。但是那只是對美國市場的刻板印象。我們可以從特殊市場切入，如住在小公寓的學生，或是獨居的老人，這些消費者不需要洗大量的衣服。而且，重點是他們的空間有限，放不下大型的家電產品。我的研究顯示，在美國市場小型家電中，我們還沒有競爭者呢。這使我相信，我們的商品正好可以滿足這特殊市場的需求。

| Joseph | Well done, Claire!! I'm glad that you did the research; it's very helpful for our subject. Submit your report to my desk before Friday, I can't wait to read through it. More research needs to be conducted before we give this project the green light, | 做得好，Claire！！我很高興妳做了研究，這對我們的計畫很有幫助。週五之前把妳的報告交出來。我迫不及待要看這份報告了。希望同事們也可以一起研究看看。 |

抓「龍」TIME

☹ The outlook is very attractive.
☺ The appearance is very attractive.
☹ Our products ZZ-123 and YY-246 are not good for the States' market.
☺ Our products ZZ-123 and YY-246 are not suitable for the States' market.

經典好用句

☺ **my opinion is that**⋯   我的看法是⋯⋯

= my point of view is that

My opinion is that you should stop seeing him

我的看法是你應該不要再跟他碰面了

☺ **as far as I'm concerned**   就我而言

As far as I'm concerned, quality is always my first priority.

對我而言，品質才是最重要的。

字彙精選

■**proposal**   *n*   提案

Your proposal of the new market development is not practical.

你新市場開發的提案看起來有點不切實際。

■**household appliance**   *n*   家用電器

A household appliance is a mechanical or electrical machine that does a particular job in the home, such as cooking or cleaning.

家用電器是指用以處理家中特定工作，像是烹飪或是清潔的機械式或是電子式的機器。

■**stereotype**   *n*   刻板印象

Generally speaking, it's a stereotype that American loves high-calorie foods.

一般來說，對於美國人的刻板印象是，他們多偏愛高熱量食物。

■ **tap into** 進軍

Japanese food had been tapped into the States restaurant for decades.

日本食物已經進軍美國餐飲業數十年。

■ **competitor** *n* 競爭對手

Apple and Samsung are competitors in the mobile market. they have legal proceedings against each other.

Apple 跟三星公司是手機市場的競爭對手，他們互相提告。

■ **submit** *v* 提交

David should submit his paper to the professor before this Saturday.

David 應該在本週六之前把報告提交給教授。

抓龍術大公開

1. The ~~outlook~~ appearance is very attractive.

外表很吸引人。

外表
☹outlook
☺appearance

outlook 應是指前景，看法。例如：
The outlook for the digital watch is uncertain.
（智能手表的前景未明。）
若我們要說明某產品的外觀，應用 appearance 這單字。

2. Our products ZZ-123 and YY-246 are not ~~good~~ suitable for the States' market.

我們的產品 ZZ-123和YY-246不適合美國市場。

不適合

☹not good for

☺not suitable for

"be not good for"應指「對……不好」，例如：

Smoking is not good for your health.

（吸菸對你的健康有礙。）

若要說明某產品不適合某市場，應用"be suitable for"– 對什麼適合。
另外要補充一點，the States' market = the US market = the market in the US。美國人常會簡稱美國為 the States。

Unit 10 會議取消

In the conference room
在會議室裡

Claire	Joseph, I'm afraid I've got a bad news; Cindy just told me that tomorrow's meeting with Mr. Yamada has to be cancelled.	Joseph，我有個壞消息要報告。Cindy剛剛跟我說明天與Yamada先生的會議必須取消了。
Joseph	Cancelled? This can't be happening! You know very well how important this meeting is. I had your guarantee two days ago. You promised me that there would be a solid performance of our elaborate team work. Are you aware of these negotiations are hanging by a thread? This cancellation might ruin our annual sales plan!!	取消？門都沒有！！妳知道這次會議的重要性吧。前兩天妳還跟我保證說在會議時能充份展現出我們優秀的團隊表現。妳知道此次會議並不容易成功吧，這次取消可能會毀了我們的年度銷售計畫。

Claire	I truly know. Please let me explain. This morning, Cindy found out the video equipment in the conference room has been damaged. We contacted with the Maintenance Department immediately. But it can't be fixed on such a short time, there's really nothing can be done.	我真的知道。請容我解釋，Cindy 今天早上發現會議室的影像設備壞了。我們即刻通知了維修部。但是不可能在這麼短時間內修好，我們實在無能為力。
Joseph	<u>You must be kidding</u>. Mr. Yamada is going to hit the roof when he hears about this. These negotiations are touch and go, this cancellation just might <u>push them over the brink</u>. Claire! I trusted you and your team.	妳開玩笑吧！！Yamada 先生知道這件事會氣壞了。我們的談判已經進行的差不多了，會議取消不就是將之前的協議推回原點嗎？Claire ！！我很信任妳跟妳的團隊的。
Claire	Sorry to say, Joseph, but there is nothing we can do so far. I've told all departments of the cancellation, and rescheduled with the client for Friday. It may not be as bad as it seems. The client agreed to a rescheduled time and didn't seem upset.	我很抱歉這樣説，但是目前我們無能為力。我已經通知所有部門關於會議取消的事了。並且也跟客戶重新約好了會議時間，就在星期五。或許事情沒有想像的糟，客戶接受了新的會議時間，看起來也沒有不開心。

Joseph	Let's hope so. I won't accept any more foul-ups on this. I have to say you and your team haven't been paying enough attention to detail on this project.	最好如此，不要再出錯了。我必須指出一點，妳的團隊在這專案上並沒有全力以赴。
Claire	I understand and accept full responsibility.	我了解，針對此事我會負起責任的。
Joseph	I'd better call Mr. Yamada again myself and offer my apologies.	我最好親自打電話給 Yamada 先生，向他道歉。
Joseph	Hello, it's Jose Chang from Goodwin. May I speak to Mr.Yamada.	你好，我是 Goodwin 公司的 Joseph Chang。請找 Yamada 先生。
Someone	Hello, I am sorry, but we don't have Yamada here. You've got the wrong number.	抱歉，我們這裡沒有 Yamada 先生，你打錯了。
Joseph	Claire!! What's going on here? It's a wrong number. I had to hang on the phone.	Claire ！！怎麼搞的。號碼不對，我只得把電話給掛了。
Claire	Let me check. I'll make a call for you.	讓我看看，我幫你撥號。

抓「龍」TIME

☹ We don't have Yamada here.
☺ There's no Yamada here.
☹ I had to hang on the phone.
☺ I had to hang up the phone.

經典好用句

☺ **you must be kidding** 你開玩笑的吧

覺得對方的說法有點可笑，或是荒謬，不可置信。這時我們可以用此句回答。表示自己不敢相信，或是覺得不可思議。

A: The bride wouldn't release her wedding photos until the photos are altered.

B: You must be kidding, that's ridiculous.

A：婚禮的相片沒有修圖過，那個新娘就不肯拿出來。

B：你開玩笑的吧，真是荒謬。

☺ **push someone over the brink** 將……逼上絕路

If you deny his application, you are pushing him over the brink.

如果你拒絕他的申請，等同將他逼上絕路。

字彙精選

■ **guarantee** *n* 保證

We guarantee that you will get a job promotion in 2 years.

我們保證你在 2 年內能得到工作升遷。

■**solid** *adj/n* 可靠的，信賴的；固體

The lawyer needs some solid evidence to prove his client is innocent.

律師需要確實的證據，證明他的委託人是無辜的。

■**elaborate** *adj* 精心製作的，講究的

Carol has devoted herself on an elaborate research project.

Carol 置身投入一項複雜的研究計畫。

■**are you aware of** 你清楚嗎？你有感覺到嗎？

I don't think that you are aware of the importance of his visiting.

我不認為你清楚他此次拜訪的重要性。

■**maintenance** *n* 保養

Many girls are not aware of car maintenance.

許多女生對汽車保養並不清楚。

■**brink** *n* 邊緣，原始狀態

Gooty spider is on the brink of extinction.

Gooty 蜘蛛面臨滅絕邊緣。

抓龍術大公開

1. ~~W e don't have~~ There is no Yamada here.

這裡沒有Yamada這個人。

當有人打錯電話時，應該說 You've got the wrong number. 若有指定找誰，但並沒這個人的時候，我們可以說

There is no one here by that name.

Part 1 會議

（這裡沒有你説的那個人。）

There's no Yamada here in this company.

（我們公司裡並沒有 Yamada 這個人。）

在電話英文當中，習慣以 This is…或是 It's…第三人稱的方式作為開頭，原因有兩種説法，第一種是認為在電話普遍化之前，當時認為以第三人稱的方式説話較有禮貌，而直接以 I'm…的方式開頭，則被認為是口氣太衝。第二種的説法則是早期電話是需要透過接線生來轉接的，所以一般習慣以第三人稱的方式來説。

2.I had to hang ~~on~~ up the phone.

我得掛電話了。

掛電話
☹hang on
☺hang up

hang on 與 hang up 對於以中文為母語的人士，容易造成混淆，因為 on 和 up 在中文裡都有「上」的含意，在這裡要注意的是 hang on 是有「堅持下去」的意思，用在講電話時，則是請對方等一下，不要掛掉電話。而 hang up 則是掛電話，停止通話之意。

如果要跟對方通知「我要掛電話」的話，則可以説"I'll have to ring off."或是"I'll have to hang up."。

例句

I'll have to ring off, my boss is coming.

我最好掛電話，我老闆來了。

Unit 11 會議不順利

David	I think that winds my presentation up and hope that you could realize why Star 1 is the top product of Goodwin.	我想我們報告就此結束，希望您能了解 Star 1 為什麼是我們公司的一線產品。
Mark	Thank you for that presentation, David. It was impressive. Unfortunately, I am afraid that we're not able to purchase your product at this movement.	謝謝你的報告，David。報告令人印象深刻。遺憾的是我們恐怕此時無法跟你採購了。
David	Wow~ now my mind is a blur. Mark, what makes you change your mind? I'd really appreciate some feedback. Can you tell me why you are no longer interested in Start 1?	哇～我完全不知道是怎麼回事。Mark, 你為什麼改變主意了？ 如果你可以告訴我原因，為什麼你們對 Star 1 不感興趣了？

Mark	I'm sure you understand how competitive the luggage industry has become. Tourism industry is getting more and more prosperous. Frankly speaking, the Star 1 doesn't stand out from the rest.	我想你知道行李箱市場是非常競爭的。觀光產業越來越蓬勃發展。但是坦白說，Star 1 並不是在此之間最突出的。
David	Why do you feel this way? Goodwin has worked very hard to produce quality luggage.	你為什麼會有此看法。Goodwin 一直致力於生產高品質行李箱。
Mark	Please don't get me wrong, David, Star 1 is an excellent product, but one of your competitors' luggage has more and better functions. More importantly, it is at a much lower price.	請別誤解我的話，David。Star 1 是很好的產品。但是你們有一家競爭對手的行李箱有更多功能，而且更重要的事，他的價格相對低廉許多。
David	If you don't mind my asking, who is that competitor?	方便透露這競爭者嗎？
Mark	Of course, I don't mind. Have you heard of a small company called Luckwin which produces the Moon 1?	當然，你有聽過一家小型廠商叫"Luckwin"，他們生產的"Moon 1"嗎？

David	Yes, I have. It's a copycat company. How long has their product been on the market and why is it so special?	當然，這是一家愛抄襲的公司。他們的產品上市多久了，有什麼特殊功能？
Mark	It's only been on the market for a few weeks. On top of what Star 1 has, it's water-resistant and dust-resistant.	這產品才上市短短幾星期，它有 Star1 所有的功能，除此之外，它能防水、耐髒。
David	I see that it has more functions. But its quality is not reliable at all. The functions is not as good as it claims. I don't consider it as a trustworthy company.	原來是因為它有更多的功能。但是它的品質一點也不可靠，而且它所宣稱的功能可能沒那麼好。我不認為這是一家值得信賴的公司。
Mark	Well, you made a good point of view. I don't want some lousy product problems to make my clients complain. ☹It will make me trouble.	你說到重點了，我不想一些二流的產品問題讓我的客戶抱怨。這會讓我惹上麻煩。
David	☹Maybe I can let it pass and start over?	或許，我們可以忘記之前討論的，然後重頭開始。

Mark　　　I'll take that under advisement.

我會鄭重考慮你的建議的。

抓「龍」TIME

☹ It will make me trouble
☺ Make trouble for me
☹ Maybe I can let it pass and start over?
☺ Maybe I can put it behind and start over?

經典好用句

☺ **I'll take... under advisement** 我會考慮將……納入考慮的

advisement 深思熟慮

Terry would take experts' suggestion under advisement, and make the right decision.

Terry 會將專家的建議納入考慮，然後做出正確決定。

☺ **don't get me wrong** 別誤會

Don't get me wrong, but I think you are make a detour.

別誤會了，但是我認為你在繞路。

字彙精選

■ **wind… up**　收尾，結束

The ceremony is about to wind up because of the bad weather.

因為天氣變糟，儀式差不多要結束了。

■ **unfortunately**　*adv*　不幸的

Unfortunately, we can't agree with your terms and condition, which will leave us no profit at all.

不幸的，我們無法同意貴公司的交易條件。那會我司毫無利潤。

■ **blur**　*n/v*　不清楚

My mind is a blur.

我的腦袋不清楚，一片空白。

■ **prosperous**　*adj*　繁榮的，富裕的

The China economic is getting more and more prosperous in the 21 centuries.

在 21 世紀，中國經濟越來越繁榮。

■ **trustworthy**　*adj*　值得信賴的

Many people will consider the Apple smartphone as a trustworthy choice.

許多人認為 Apple 手機是值得信賴的選擇。

■ **lousy**　*adj*　討人厭的,令人不舒服的。

Alan and Karen went to a famous restaurant for the anniversary; however, the lousy food there just ruined celebration.

Alan 和 Karen 去一家知名餐廳慶祝他們的周年紀念日，但是那裡糟糕的食物毀了一切。

抓龍術大公開

1. ~~It will make me trouble.~~ Make Trouble for me.
替我找麻煩。

☹It will make me trouble

☺Make trouble for me

make trouble for sb - 造成某人的麻煩

例句

You should behavior yourself; don't make trouble for your parents.
你應該守規矩，不要給你父母找麻煩。

2. Maybe I can ~~let it pass~~ put it behind and start over?
或許，我們可以忘記之前討論的，然後重頭開始。

讓這事情過去

☹let it pass

☺put it behind

這一句也可以說成"**Let bygones be bygones.**"（讓過去的事成為過去、既往不咎）。

bygones　n　過去的事（多意指不愉快的事）

例句

Let bygones be bygones, we should move on.
過去的不愉快就算了吧，我們得向前看。

Unit 12　職務變動

| Joseph | We are about to start the meeting. I am aware that there is a strong difference of opinion regarding this subject, but we need to come to a consensus on who is the best one to take the position of the sales manager. My vote is for Claire from sales department. | 會議差不多要開始了。我知道我們對於此議題意見分歧,但是我們需要就誰適任業務經理一事達成共識。我投票給業務部的 Claire。 |

David	I completely disagree. I found Claire is a little hard-headed. It's difficult to communicate with her. Cindy would be far better at keeping the Sales Department motivated and surpassing sales targets. In fact, Cindy just won our first Japan client last month, that's a huge success. Therefore, I believe that Cindy is <u>head and shoulders above</u> the rest.	我不贊成。我覺得 Claire 有點難相處，而且很難跟她溝通。在激勵跟超越業務目標上，Cindy 一直表現得很好。事實上，Cindy 上個月才拿下一家日本客戶，這是了不起的成就。我相信 Cindy 在所有之中是最棒的。
Sophia	Well, we are thrilled that Cindy got Toyo's business. But she has just joined us for 6 months. I've worked with Cindy, and I don't think she is ready for a management position. Claire, on the other hand, she has worked in Goodwin for over 3 years. I believe that she is the most ideal candidate for this position.	嗯，對於 Cindy 拿下 Toyo 公司的生意，我們都很興奮。但是她才來公司六個月。我跟 Cindy 工作過，我不認為她目前有能力接下管理的職位。另一面，Claire 就做的不錯，她在我們公司待 3 年了，我想她是最理想的人選。

Joseph David, I agree that Cindy is an ambitious and capable young lady. But you have to take seniority into consideration. Clare has more international business experiences; she has been doing her job very well, and most important thing is our clients like her. I think we'd be making a mistake if we appointed Cindy as the new manager.

David，我同意 Cindy 是個有野心且有能力的年輕姑娘。但是你必須把年資考慮進去。Claire 有更多的國際商業經驗，她的表現一直都很好。最重要的是，我們的客戶都喜歡她。如果我們選 Cindy 做了業務經理，我覺得那會是個錯誤的決定。

David Ok, it seems that there is a lot of disagreement on this matter. I know you don't think Cindy is the best candidate for this position. But I beg to differ. However, I'm willing to also consider Claire as the new manager.

看來真是我們有很大的意見不同，我知道你們不認為 Cindy 是適合的人選。但我不認同此點。不過，我也是可是考慮 Claire 來做業務經理的。

Joseph	I think it's time we put the matter to a vote. All those in favor of appointing Claire as manager, please raise your hands. Well, it looks like most people agree that Claire is the best choice. We should release the appointment and offer her more pay next month.	我想是時候該投票了。認為 Claire 可當經理的，請舉手。看來大家都同意 Claire 是最好的選擇了。我們應該公布此任命並下個月開始給她調薪。

抓「龍」TIME

☹ Offer her more pay next month

☺ Offer her a pay raise next month.

經典好用句

☺ **head and shoulders above** 比……棒多了，脫穎而出

For Rick and Lori, their son stands head and shoulders above any other kids. 就 Rick 和 Lori 而言，他們的兒子比其他孩子棒多了。

☺ **beg to differ** 恕難認同

A: We should fire John ASAP, he is a trouble maker.

B: I bet to differ.

A：我們應該盡快將 John 解職，他一直惹麻煩。

B：恕難認同。

字彙精選

■ **regarding** *prep* 有關

Don't hesitate to contact with us, if you have any questions regarding the sample. 若你對樣品有任何疑問，請儘管跟我聯繫。

■ **consensus** *n* 共識

There is a growing consensus on the air pollution issue. 在空氣汙染議題上逐漸有了共識。

■ **hard-headed** *adj* 頑固的

Stephan is hard-headed; he can't get along well with his friends.
Stephan 很頑固，他跟朋友相處不來。

■ **motivate** *v* 激發，給……動機

The new policy was designed to motivate students to study more efficiently.
新的政策是設計讓學生學習更有效率。

■ **ideal** *adj* 理想的

An ideal husband doesn't exist in the reality.
理想的丈夫在現實中並不存在。

■ **disagreement** *n* 分歧，意見不合

Jack and Ivan have some disagreement on the earphone promotion plan.
Jack 跟 Ivan 在耳機行銷計畫上意見不合。

抓龍術大公開

1. Offer her ~~more pay~~ a pay raise next month
我們下個月給她加薪

加薪
☹more pay
☺pay raise

「加薪」用 more pay，在文法中並無不妥，這裡的 pay 當名詞的「薪資、酬勞」使用，但一般在英文句子當中，用到 more pay，主詞大多是勞方。而這一句的主詞為資方，提供加薪的機會，應用 pay raise（可用在勞資雙方）較為恰當。

例句

我想要加薪。

Could you give me a raise?

= I'd like to have a chance of a pay raise.

= I want to have a pay raise.

A: I got a pay raise

B: Great !! Let's celebrate it.

A: 我加薪了

B: 很好，我們去慶祝吧

Part II

文件
Document

Unit 1 延後出貨

E-mail 1

Dear Jack

We are hereby to <u>call your attention to</u> the delay of order #2006. The subject goods reached London on 16 Feb, which is almost 2 weeks late from our contract. In the PO, the ETA was supposed to be 02 Feb. <u>To our regret</u>, we have to inform you that we can't accept those delay goods.

From the beginning of our communication, we had stressed that the delivery date was crucial. We must receive the goods before the Commercial Digital Show Starts, which was 10 Feb. And you also promised us on the delivery. Now, the goods are completely late for the show. We lost a great opportunity to promote those earphones. To compensate our loss, we claim 30 % discount of the payment.

Please reply to our claim immediately, at the same time, we also hold the payment to this decision.

Regards/ Warren

E-mail 1

尊敬的 Jack

我們在此必須向你提出關於訂單 #2006 延誤的客訴。此單貨物於 2 月 16 日抵達倫敦，這日期足足比我們合約所記載的晚了兩星期。在訂購單上，貨物本預計是 2 月 2 日要到送達的。很遺憾的，我們必須在此通知貴公司，此批延遲的貨物，我司不接受。

在一開始我們雙方溝通時，我方強調交期十分重要，必須在數位電子展開始前收到此批貨物，而電子展的日期是 2 月 10 號。貴公司當初也承諾能如期交貨。現在貨物已經完全趕不上電子展了。我方喪失了推銷此耳機的大好機會。為了彌補我們損失，我們要求付款折價 **30%**

請即刻針對我方的訴求做出回應，同時，我們此筆貨款我方亦暫時扣留。

Warren
敬上

E-mail 2

Dear Warren

Thanks for your email.

We are very sorry to hear that the goods are delayed for the show.

About your claim, we found maybe the delay was caused by the modified design. In a fact, after receiving your order, the earphone design was modified twice as your request. I'm sure you can understand that we were unable to manufacture the goods without the final design drawing.

However, for the long term cooperation, we would accept 7% discount of this payment. We hope that you will be satisfied with the resolution.

Thank you.

Regards/ Jack

E-mail 2

尊敬的 Warren

謝謝你的來信

我們很抱歉聽到貨物趕不上電子展。

關於您的客訴。我們認為或許延誤是因為更改產品設計有關。事實上，在收到訂單之後，依照貴公司的要求，耳機的設計變更了兩次。我想貴公司應該很清楚，在設計沒有定稿之前，我們是無法安排生產貨物的。

然而，為了長期的合作關係。我們願意提供 **7%** 的折扣給您做為補償。希望您能滿意這樣的結果。

致上敬意
Jack

Part II 文件

Dialogue

Ivan	Hey, Jack, I heard about Warren's claim. Is everything ok?	嘿，Jack。 我聽說 Warren 的客訴了，處理的怎樣了？
Jack	Warren had modified the design twice, and I reminded him that the delivery would be delayed. But, he said they would arrange the air freight then. Now, he wanted to claim on the delivery? That's ridiculous! Anyway, I already replied him. It's impossible to accept 30% discount, 7% is fair enough. I don't feel well about it.	Warren 改了二次設計，而且我還提醒他這樣交期會延誤。他說他們到時候要走空運。現在他跟我客訴交期？太奇怪了。總之，不可能同意他折價 30%，最多只能給他 7%。這事我處理好了。但是我還是很不開心吶。
Ivan	I agree with you. Listen, I have a meeting with my dentist this afternoon. Can you cover my swift?	你說得沒錯。ㄟ，我下午跟牙醫有約。你幫我代班好嗎？
Jack	No problem.	沒問題啦。

抓「龍」TIME

☹ I don't feel well about it.
☺ I am upset about it.
☹ I have a meeting with my dentist this afternoon.
☺ I have an appointment with my dentist this afternoon.

經典好用句

Part II 文件

☺ **call attention to**　特此告知；喚起注意

The report has called public attention to the air pollution problem.
這份報告引起大眾對空氣污染的重視

☺ **to our regret**　很遺憾的……

To our regret all the photos in the computer are lost.
很遺憾的電腦裡的照片都遺失了。

字彙精選

■ **crucial**　*adj*　重要的

Rick is crucial for us, we can't survive without him.
Rick 對我們很重要，沒有他，我們沒辦法存活。

■ **completely**　*adv*　完全的，徹底的

Living abroad is not easy, it's completely different from our experience.
在國外生活不容易，跟我們之前的經驗完全不同。

■**compensate** *v* 補償

Your company should compensate for your business travelling cost in Finland

你們公司應該要補償你出差芬蘭的費用。

■**claim** *v/n* 客訴，索賠，主張

The lady claimed US$1,000 for the accident in restaurant.

那位女士因為餐廳的意外事件，要求 US$1,000 的賠償。

■**modify** *v* 修改

The toy company had modified the design, now the new toy car is safer for children.

玩具公司修改了設計，現在新的玩具車對兒童來說更安全了。

■**resolution** *n* 決議

A resolution is a formal decision. You should respect it.

決議為一正式的決定，因此你應該遵守。

抓龍術大公開

1.I ~~don't feel well~~ am upset about it.

我還是很不開心吶。

不舒服（心理上）
☹don't feel well
☺upset

在情境對話中，Jack 想表達的是，針對客戶這件事覺得不舒服，不開心。而不是 Jack 生病了。而 don't feel well，是指生病了，是生理上

的不舒服。而用以形容心理上的不舒服，應用 upset 或是 depressed。

例句

I am upset about what Seven said.
Seven 講的話讓我不舒服（心理）。

2.I have ~~a meeting~~ an appointment with my dentist this afternoon.
我下午跟牙醫有約。

預約
☹meeting
☺appointment

meeting 指的是會議，而在對話中與牙醫的約應該被解釋成預約，
所以要説 appointment，這一句也可以説成"I have a dentist
appointment this afternoon."。以下為常見的幾種易搞混的「約」的
例句。

例句

I have an appointment with my dentist next Friday.
我下週五跟牙醫有約。（看牙）
I have a date with my dentist next Friday.
我下週五跟牙醫有約。（約會）
I have a meeting with my dentist next Friday.
我下週五跟牙醫要開會

Part II 文件

Unit 2 代理徵求

E-mail 1

Dear Sir

This is Vasa Company from Sweden. We attended the recently held a digital component show in Taipei last week and were impressed by the high quality, attractive design, and reasonable price of your earphones. We have seen your full catalogue and are convinced that there is a promising market here in Sweden for your products. If, as we presume, you are not yet represented here, we should be interested in acting as your sole agent in Sweden.

Vasa, as a leading importer and distributor in consumer electronics product for more than 10 years, we have a good knowledge of the Sweden market and have fostered a close business relationship with the domestic wholesalers. We feel confident that if you offer us the opportunity to deal in your earphones. The result will be entirely satisfactory to both of us.

We firmly believe that an agency for marketing your products in Sweden would be of a considerable benefit to you.

Please let us know your quotation, the rate of our commission, and payment terms, so that we may begin negotiating with our customers to secure their orders.

E-mail 1

Looking forward to hearing from you soon.
Thank you.
Regards / Henk

敬啟者

我們是瑞典的 **VASA** 公司，上週我們在台北參加了電子零件展。貴司的耳機高品質，吸引人的設計及合理的價格我們印象深刻。我們拿到貴司的全套目錄，我們相信貴司的耳機在瑞典市場一定會大受歡迎。若貴司在瑞典尚未有代理商，我們十分樂意成為貴司在瑞典的代理商。

我們公司 **Vasa**，在消費性電子產品中已經有超過 **10** 年，一直是領先的進口商及經銷商。並跟當地零售商培養保持良好關係。若貴司能考慮將您的耳機由我公司代理，我們相信結果會很令人滿意的。我們深切的相信這份瑞典的代理合約，將會為貴司帶來可觀的利潤。請提供報價，佣金比例，付款條件等。如此，我們可以開始與客戶洽談訂購事項。

希望早日收到您的回覆。
謝謝

致上敬意 / Henk

Part II 文件

Dialogue

Jack	Ivan, I received a letter from Stockholm, Sweden.	Ivan，我收到一封來自瑞典，斯德哥爾摩的信。
Ivan	<u>As far as I know</u>, we don't have client in Sweden. Can you double confirm it?	就我所知，我們沒有瑞典的客人，你能再確認一次嗎？
Jack	I did. It's Vasa, they attended the show last week in Taipei, and they love our earphone and want to be our agent in Sweden.	確認過了是 Vasa，他們上週參加台北的電子展。很喜歡我們的耳機，想要瑞典代理權。
Ivan	Well, we should meet with them then make the decision. Where is Seven? We need to discuss on this subject.	那我們應該要先和他們碰面，才能決定。Seven 去哪裡了？我們來討論此事。
Jack	He is out of work, it's past 5PM. I'm a glutton for work.	他下班了，已經過五點了。我是工作狂。

Ivan	We both are. Get your passport ready, you and I will need to go to Stockholm next week.	我們兩個都是，把你護照準備一下，我們下週去斯德哥爾摩一趟。
Jack	<u>I'm right on it.</u>	馬上去辦。

抓「龍」TIME

☹ Can you re-confirm it?

☺ Can you check it again?

☹ He is out of work.

☺ He has got off work.

經典好用句

☺ **as far as I know**　就我所知

As far as I know, they had spent much counsel fee on lawsuit.

就我所知，他們在法律訴訟案上花費很多。

☺ **I'm right on it.**　我這就去辦

A: John, can you cancel my flight? I won't go to Tokyo tomorrow.

B: I'm right on it.

A：John，可以幫我取消航班嗎？我明天不去東京了。

B：我這就去辦。

字彙精選

■ **convinced** *adj* 深信的

The parents were convinced that the teacher was doing the right thing.

家長們都很相信老師所作所為。

■ **presume** *v* 假設

I presume that you don't want to go out with Darren, why don't you just reject him.

我猜你根本不想跟 Darren 出去，你為什麼不拒絕他？

■ **electronics** *n* 電子

Many girls are not interested in electronics.

許多女生對電子產品不感興趣。

■ **foster** *v* 培養

The air pollution has been fostered by expanding heavy industry.

重工業的擴張造成空氣汙染。

■ **domestic** *adj* 國內的

Because of the slump in the domestic demand, firms begin to export the product.

因為國內的需求大幅下降，公司開始外銷產品。

■ **considerable** *adj* 值得考慮的

I think his suggestion is considerable, in this way, the customer will stop complaining about our service.

我認為他的建議值得考慮。如此一來，客戶便不再抱怨我們的服務。

Part II 文件

抓龍術大公開

1. Can you ~~double confirm~~ check it again?
可以再確認一次嗎？

再確認
☹double confirm
☺check again?

常聽到的 **double confirm** 其實是錯誤用法，然而已經太常出現我們日常生活中，讓人難注意到其實是錯誤的。正確說法可以加 **re-**（重複），以 **re-confirm**（再確認），或是直接在原句加上 **again**，如 **check again**，這樣是比較恰當的。

例句

Can you check my flight again? I'm not sure the flight no is CI626 or CI262.
可以幫我再查一下我們航班嗎？我不確定編號是 **CI626** 或是 **CI262**。

2. He ~~is out of~~ has got off **work.**

他下班了。

下班
☹out of work
☺get off work

out of work，正確的解釋為他沒有工作了，並不單單是下班而已。下班一般可以說 get off work，get off duty，leave the office 等，也可以用形容打卡下班的方式，如 clock out，punch out 來表示下班。

例句

 A: Hi, may I speak to Maggie?
 B: She already left the office.
 A：請問 Maggie 在嗎？
 B：她下班了哦。

Part II 文件

Unit 3　通知拜訪

E-mail 1

Hi, Henk

It's Jack from Inno Corp.

Thank you for the letter of April 4 and we are pleased to know that you like our earphone.

Our company, Inno, established in 2012, it's a young company, but expanded rapidly for the past 2 years. At present, our overseas agents are mainly in North American and Asia. There are signs of a promising market for our products and we believe an active agent could bring a big increase in our sales volume. Therefore, we are attracted by the chance to develop our trade further afield and are interested in your proposal.

We appreciate your suggestion of acting as our sole agency in Sweden, but, first of all, we would like to know the approximate quantity of your target annual sales volume. And when sufficient mutual understanding is attained between us, we shall revert to this issue. Therefore, my co-worker and I would like to visit you next week if it's convenient for you. By this visiting, we can understand of each other and discuss the further cooperation details.

Please advise.

E-mail 1

Thank you.
Regards/ Jack
Henk 您好

本人為 Inno 的 Jack

謝謝您於四月四號時的來信,我們很榮幸您喜歡我司的耳機。
我們公司,Inno,成立於 2012 年是個很新的公司,但是在過去兩年裡成長快速。我們目前的代理商主要是在北美及亞洲地區,從這種跡象顯示,我們的產品前景可期。我們相信,有能力的代理商能夠將大幅增加我司產品銷售。因此,對於貴公司的提議,我們十分有興趣,也希望有此機會能擴展貿易。

十分感謝您的提議。不過,首先,我們想知道貴公司預估在瑞典市場上,我司產品的一年銷售量。此外,在討論代理權之前,我司希望能與貴公司有充分互相的認識。

因此,如果方便的話,我的同事與我決定下週去拜訪貴公司。藉此,我們可以互相了解,並就合作細節詳細討論。

請您回覆
謝謝
Jack 敬上

Dialogue

Jack	Gabriel, I received a letter from Sweden yesterday, it's a new company, Vasa, and they want our sole agency in Sweden. After discussing with Ivan yesterday, we decided to go to Sweden next week.	Gabriel，昨天我們收到一封來自瑞典的信，一間新公司，VASA，他們想做我們的瑞典獨家代理。我跟 Ivan 昨天討論過了，我們下週要去瑞典一趟。
Gabriel	Sweden? That's near Denmark. You should stop by Copenhagen and visit Mermaid. Their annual quantity is about 10,000 pcs.	瑞典，那離丹麥很近，你們要順便去哥本哈根拜訪 Mermaid 公司嗎？他們的年銷售 10,000 個耳機。
Jack	Yep, we will. So, I need to finish that market analysis before this Friday. But my computer is broken.	會去。所以我得在週五前把這市場分析報告完成。但是我的電腦壞了。
Gabriel	Don't worry. It happens. You can use mine. Are you ok? You look exhausted.	別擔心，有時候會發生這種事。你可以用我的電腦。你還好嗎？你看起來好累。
Jack	Well, I have extra work for 2 days. I should leave office earlier today and get some rest.	我已經加班兩天了，我今天應該早點回去休息。

抓「龍」TIME

☹ But my computer is broken.

☺ But my computer is out of order.

☹ I have extra work for 2 days.

☺ I have worked overtime for 2 days.

經典好用句

☺ **it happens** 常有的事

遇到不順心的事，對方會說此句，表示希望你能想開一點，不要放在心上。

A: I left my phone in the restaurant.

B: Don't worry, it happens. I'm sure we can find it.

A：我把手機留在餐廳裡。

B：別擔心，常有的事，我們可以找到的。

☺ **you look exhausted** 你看起來很累

用到 exhausted 此字表示精疲力竭，比 tired 累，就程度上來說，是還要累很多。

A: What happened? You look exhausted.

B: I haven't slept for 2 days.

A：發生了什麼事？你看起來精疲力竭。

B：我已經兩天沒睡了。

字彙精選

■ **rapidly** *adv* 很快的，迅速的

The population of China is rapidly growing; therefore, the government has developed the population plan.

中國人口成長迅速，因此政府展開了人口計畫。

■ **approximate** *adj* 大約的

The approximate price of new product varies from $ 250-$300

新產品的價格約為 US$250-US$300 之間。

■ **attain** *v* 達到

It's impressive the students made lots effort to attain their goal.

學生努力的達成目標讓人感動

■ **revert** *v* 恢復原狀

After hours of repairing, the toy was reverted to type.

經過幾個小時的修復，那玩具已經恢復原狀。

■ **further** *adj* 進一步的

We are waiting for the further instruction from the embassy.

我們正在等大使館的進一步指示。

抓龍術大公開

1. But my computer is ~~broken~~ out of order.

我的電腦故障了

故障
☹broken
☺out of order

用 **broken** 來形容，則是說我電腦摔壞。但是對話中，**Jack** 想說的是，他的電腦不能用了。所以應用 **out of order** 較為貼切。

例句

The ticket vendor is out of order, you should try another one.
那台售票機故障了，你應該試別台看看。

2. I have ~~extra work~~ worked overtime for 2 days.
我已經加班兩天

加班
☹extra work
☺work overtime

extra work 指的是額外的工作，但是並不一定代表示加班完成，這樣的說法，意思有些不清楚。為避免混淆，「加班」請說 **work overtime**（工作超時）。

例句

I worked overtime yesterday.
我昨天加班。

Unit 4 工作通知

E-mail 1

Dear Miss Meredith

It was a pleasure to meet with you last month.

We are very impressed with your brilliant ideas about the medical equipment industry and your creative suggestions for the growth of Grey Product. After discussing with our director, Dr. Webber, I am delighted to confirm your employment as a full-time sales representative with Grey Product effective Monday, April 9.

In this position, you will be reporting to Dr. Webber, the head of our Sales department, and your responsibility will include new market development and product promotion for the international market.

We would like to offer you a salary of USD$5,000/ month. As an employee, <u>you will be eligible for</u> salary increases based upon your performance and length of service, 2 weeks paid vacation, participation in the company retirement plan, and the stock options in Grey product. We can discuss the detail benefits in person if you are interested in accepting the position.

Please take this offer under serious consideration, and

E-mail 1

reply by Feb 16. Our orientation will be launched from March 1 to March 10.

We are looking forward to working with you here at Grey Product, and we are pleased to have you in our team.

Regards/ Izzie

Human Resource Department

親愛的 Meredith 小姐

很高興上週跟你碰面。

您對於醫療器材產業獨特的見解跟對我們公司充滿創意的建議讓我們印象深刻。跟我們老闆討論之後，我很榮幸的通知您從 4 月 9 日星期一起，您將成為我們公司的全職業務代表。

在此職位，您的直屬主管為 Dr. Webber，業務部門的領導，您將負責國際市場的新市場開發跟產品促銷。

我們提供給您 USD$5,000 的月薪。做為 Grey 公司的員工，您的薪資將依工作表現，服務年資而增加，並享有兩週的帶薪假期，參與公司的退休計畫及公司的認股權。如果您願意接受我們公司的工作，我們可再面對面來討論服其他福利的細節。

請您慎重考慮我們公司的提議，並於 2 月 16 日前回覆。我們的新人培訓將於 3 月 1 日開始至 3 月 10 日。

歡迎你加入我們的團隊，期待能與您在 Grey 共事

致上敬意 / Izzie

人力資源部門

Dialogue

Meredith	Hey, Stephan, I got the job acceptance letter from Grey Product. <u>I can't believe it</u>, I had heard that there were dozens people applied for the job vacancy and been worried for a while. After all, medical equipment is a totally new field for me.	嘿，Stephen， 我收到 Grey 公司的錄取通知了，真是不敢相信。聽説有好幾十人應徵這個職位，我擔心了好一陣子。畢竟，醫療設備對我來説是個全新的領域。
Stephen	Fantastic!! It's your dream job. I'm happy for you.	太好了，這是你夢想中的工作，真替妳開心。
Meredith	Thanks, listen, <u>I need to change my work today. Can you replace me this afternoon?</u> I need to buy some decent outfits for the orientation next week.	謝啦。 嘿，我需要換班，你今天下午可以幫我代班嗎？ 我要去買幾件好衣服參加新進員工培訓。
Stephen	Sure! Not a problem.	當然，有什麼問題。

抓「龍」TIME

☹ I need to change my work today.
☺ I need to change the swift today.
☹ Can you replace me this afternoon?
☺ Can you cover for me this afternoon?

經典好用句

☺ **you will be eligible for** 你將有資格……

Rick and his family will be eligible for the new community residency.
Rick 跟他的家人將有資格獲得新社區的居住權。

☺ **I can't believe it** 真不敢相信

A: The China government rejected his visa application.
B: I can't believe it.
A：中國政府拒絕他的簽證申請。
B：真不敢相信。

字彙精選

■ **employment** *n* 雇用，任職

The new employment laws will eliminate sex discrimination.
新就業法將會消除性別歧視。

Part II 文件

■ **effective** *adj* 有效的

The WHO expects that the new vaccine will be effective against the Ebola virus.

世界衛生組織期待新的疫苗能有效的對抗伊波拉病毒。

■ **participation** *n* 參與

Without Terry's participation, we can't convene the annual general meeting.

沒有 Terry 的參與，年度大會無法召開。

■ **stock options** 認股權

Many companies have stock options for their employee.

許多公司都有員工認股權。

■ **orientation** *n* 新人培訓，方向

They give their new employees a week orientation.

他們給新進員工進行了一星期的新人培訓。

■ **decent** *adj* 像樣的，得體的（多為形容服裝）

I need some decent outfits for my job interview next week.

下星期要面試了，我需要幾件得體的衣服。

抓龍術大公開

1. I need to change ~~my work~~ the shift today.

我今天要換班。

換班
☹change the work
☺change the shift

change my work，依字面應解釋成為更換工作，有換職位的含意，但在對話中為要更動上班的時間，也就是中文裡的換班，這樣的工作時間調度應說是 change the shift。

例句

> A: I need to go to bank tomorrow; can I change the swift with you?
> B: Sure, no problem.
> A：我明天要去銀行，可以跟你換班嗎？
> B：好的，沒問題。

2. Can you ~~replace~~ cover for me this afternoon?
今天下午可以幫我代班嗎？

代班
☹replace
☺cover for

代班的正確說法應用 "cover for"。

例句

> A: There is big sale in the mall, can you cover for me this afternoon.
> B: Don't be silly.
> A：商場在折扣了，你下午幫我代班好嗎？
> B：別傻了。

Unit 5 代理

Dear Sir,

We are Travel King from South Africa; we would like to inform you that we act on a sole agency basis for a number of manufacturers. We specialize in luggage for Africa market. So far, we have been working with over 10 different brands luggage manufactures and our collaboration has proven to be mutually beneficial. Please refer to the attached files; those are the information regarding our company. After reading that information, you will have a detailed idea about our company.

Last week, we had attended LA Travel Exhibition and met with Mr. Joseph Chang there. We are very interested in an exclusive arrangement with your new item, Star 1.

We like to promote it in our South Africa market. It's time for us to cooperate with each other.

Looking forward to hearing from you soon.

Regards/ Jon Lester

Travel King

E-mail 1

您好

我們是來自南非的 Travel King 公司，我們是許多廠商的獨立代理，我們為南非市場代理各式樣的行李箱。目前，我們已代理了超過 10 個不同品牌的行李箱，我們合作的廠商都一直都互利共享。請參看附檔，這些是關於我們公司的資訊。在您閱讀之後，您將對我公司有更一步的了解。

上週，我們參加了在 LA 的旅遊展，在貴公司的攤位與 Jose Chang 會談甚久。

我們對貴公司的新產品，星辰一號十分有興趣。希望能取得獨家代理。 希望能在南非市場上銷售此產品，此時，是我們合作的良機。

期待您的早日回覆

致上敬意
Jon Lester
Travel King

Dialogue

David	Hi, Joseph, I received many inquiries after the exhibition. All buyers are very interested in Star 1. I guess we can say we made a good start. In addition, there was a proposal of being our agency in South Africa yesterday.	Joseph，自從上次參展之後，我每天收到許多詢價單。所有的買主對星辰一號都十分有興趣。可以説我們得到了一個好的開始。對了，我收到一封提議，有公司想要我們的南非代理權。
Joseph	South Africa? Which company?	南非？是哪家公司？
David	It's Travel King in South Africa.	是南非的 Travel King。
Joseph	I remember this company; I spoke with Jon Lester in the LA Exhibition last week. He asked me about the sole agent then. But I told him we have to consider it.	我記得這家公司，上星期在 LA 展覽時，我跟他們公司的 Jon Lester 碰面過。那時候，他跟我提過獨家代理權。我跟他説我還要再考慮看看。
Joseph	Any suggestions? I would like to know your opinion.	你有什麼建議嗎？我想聽聽你的説法。

David	Well, the Star 1 is so popular in the market. We can increase our sales scales easily. My opinion is we can cooperate with Travel King, but without releasing the sole agency to them.	星辰一號在市場上很受歡迎。我們很容易就可以增加營業額。我的意見是，我們可以跟 Travel King 合作，但是無須給他獨家代理權。
Joseph	You've made a good point. As a matter of fact, it's not right time. So, we cannot appoint any company as our sole agent.	你講到重點了。事實上，時機尚未成熟，我們不能給任何一家公司代理權。

抓「龍」TIME

☹ It's not right time.
☺ It's not the right time.

經典好用句

☺ **It's time for us to…** 我們做某事的好時機

It's time for Sb to… 某某人的好機會
It's time for Claire to get close to Jackson
這是 Claire 接近 Jackson 的好機會

☺ **make a good point** 說到重點

You made a good point; the truth is that I don't even want to visit them.
你說的很對，事實上我根本不想去拜訪他們。

字彙精選

■ **specialize in** *v* 專精於

Most students don't expect to specialize in economics.
多數學生並不專精於經濟學

■ **proven** **prove**的過去分詞；證明

Facts have proven that USA-Japan relationship is mutually beneficial.
事實證明美日關係是相互有利的。

■ **mutually beneficial** 相互利益

Jon and Keith are vendor and buyer. Their relationship is mutually beneficial.
Jon 和 Keith 是賣家跟買方，他們的關係是互利的。

■ **sole agent** 獨家代理

We have been appointed the sole agent in Denmark for the Grey Product.
我們被指為 Grey 公司的丹麥獨家代理。

■ **suggestion** *n* 建議

Jack made up his mind; he wouldn't take any suggestion from other people.
Jack 下定主意之後，就不接受別人的建議了。

■ **appoint** *v* 指定

They appointed Jack as the new technology department manager.
他們指定 Jack 為新技術部門經理。

抓龍術大公開

1. It's not the right time.
時機不對。

對的時機
☹ right time
☺ the right time

對的，你沒有看錯，這裡要解說的常見錯誤就是 **the**。在慣用英文之後，常會不小心忽略到這一個小細節，然而，有沒有 **the** 其實還蠻重要的，對於 **the** 的一般用法解釋為其為定冠詞，用在表限定、特定的名詞前，例如是 **in the USA**。但這時候應該有人會提到曾看過有人寫 **in USA**，這只能說語言除了其文法規則之外，還有約定俗成的規則。所以這方面只能靠多看、多聽、多學才是王道。

有關時機不對還有幾種說法，可以說：

The timing is not appropriate.
= The time is inappropriate.

時機不恰當。

appropriate　恰當的
inappropriate　不切當的

例句

The timing is not appropriate for party; Timmy just got fired.
Timmy 剛被解雇，現在不是開派對的好時機。

 Unit 6 開發信

E-mail 1

Dear Sir

Your company name has been given to us by AsiaTrade. com as a prospective buyer of the Japanese fabric industry. As this item is the main product of our business activities, <u>we shall be pleased</u> if we could enter into a direct business relationship with your company.

Our company, Goodwin, has been in the fabric industry for over 20 year. We are the fabric specialist. 😟<u>We manufacture all kinds of quality fabric for bags and luggage, and export to world everywhere,</u> such as the United States, Egypt, South Africa and France. We have good reputation in this field, our customers trust us as a reliable business partner.

To give you a general idea about our various kind fabric goods, we enclose a brochure in the email. Besides our regular product range, 😟<u>we also supply goods specially manufactured follow buyers' requirement.</u> Quotations and sample units will be sent to you upon receipt of your specific inquiry.

We look forward to your reply.

Regards/ Cindy

Goodwin Corp.

E-mail 1

您好

我們從 AsiaTrade.com 得知貴公司在日本是主要的織布進口商。這項產品是敝司的主要產品，我們希望有這榮幸與貴公司合作。

我們公司 GoodWin 從事織布業已經超過 20 年了，是織布業的領先專業者。我們生產各式樣的高品質行李箱與背包的織布，並行銷各地。包括：美國，埃及，南非跟法國。我們在業界享有良好的名聲，深受客戶信賴。

附上的手冊，您可了解我公司所提供的產品。除了一般的標準供貨之外，我們亦接受客戶訂製的訂單。請您告知您所需要的產品型號，我們會即刻為您提供樣品及報價單。

期待您的回覆

Cindy 敬上

Dialogue

Claire	Hey! Cindy, about the new market development program we had discussed, did you do the market research? Which company is the target at the beginning?	嘿，Cindy。我們上次討論的新市場開發計畫。研究做得如何？你有找到目標公司了嗎？
Cindy	Well, I checked the Japan Fabric import company list, and found out the Toyo's is one of the biggest fabric importer in the market. They imported about 35X20" containers Nylon fabric last year. I would like to start from this company.	我查了日本織布進口公司名單，找到 Toyo 是日本織布的重要進口公司。他們去年就進口 35 個 20 呎貨櫃的尼龍布。我想從這家公司試試看。
Claire	Good job!! I'm glad you did the research. That's a good start.	做的好，很高興妳做了研究。這是個好的開始。

Cindy	Actually, I emailed to their import department last week in which I introduced our company and products. But, I haven't gotten any reply from Toyo yet.	事實上，我上週就寫信給 Toyo 的進口部了，信中介紹了我們公司。不過，還沒得到他們的回覆。
Claire	It's always not easy to develop the new customer; it takes lots of time and patience. Keep me posted. Let me know if you need any advice.	開發新客戶是件不容易的事，需要很多時間跟耐心。有任何進度再告訴我，如果需要建議的話，隨時來找我。

Part II 文件

抓「龍」TIME

☹ We manufacture all kinds of quality fabric for bags and luggage, and export to world everywhere.

☺ We manufacture all kinds of quality fabric for bags and luggage, and export worldwide.

☹ We also supply goods specially manufactured follow buyers' requirement.

☺ We also supply goods specially manufactured according to buyers' requirement.

經典好用句

☺ **we shall be pleased to** 我們很樂意……

商業英文中，客氣的表示 我們很樂意……

We shall be pleased to establish the cooperation with your company.

我們很樂意跟貴公司建立合作關係。

☺ **keep me posted** 有任何進度，讓我知道

post 原為發布消息的意思，發展出 keep me posted 十分的口語，簡短，但卻實用。

Keep me posted. I don't want to miss any information.

有任何進度，讓我知道。我不想錯過任何消息。

字彙精選

■ **prospective** *adj* 有遠景的；預期的

The prospective study of China economy of 2016 is published today.

中國 2016 年的經濟前景調查今日出版。

■ **reputation** *n* 名聲（良好的）

Mr. Lee has a very good reputation in Chinese world, due to his devotion to the country.

因為對國家的無私貢獻，李先生在華人世界裡享有良好的名聲。

■ **enclose** *v* 附上

I enclose herewith a check for USD$200.

隨信附上支票 200 美元

■ **regular** *adj* 一般的，規律的

To keep health, you need regular work and rest time.

為了保持健康，你需要正常的工作跟休息時間。

■ **actually** *adv* 事實上

John isn't showing up today. Actually, he resigned yesterday.

John 今天沒來辦公室，事實上，他昨天就離職了。

■ **introduce** *v* 介紹

The new product was introduced to the market last month, but the customer seems not interested in it.

上個月，新的產品引入了市場。但是客戶似乎對它沒什麼興趣。

Part II 文件

抓龍術大公開

1. We manufacture all kinds of quality fabric for bags and luggage, and export ~~to world everywhere~~ worldwide.

我們生產各式各樣的高品質行李箱及背包的織布，並行銷各地。

全世界
☹world everywhere
☺worldwide

worldwide adv　遍及全球地；形容全世界還可以說是 around the world 或是 all over the world。

例句

We have 24 branch offices around the world.
我們在世界各地有 24 個辦公室。

Many people are suffering from the famine all over the world.
世界上，有需多人正在遭受飢荒。

2. We also supply goods specially manufactured ~~follow~~ according to buyers' requirement.
我們亦接受客戶訂製的訂單。

依照
☹follow
☺according to

follow 比較多的意思為跟隨，如"Follow me, I'll show you the way."（跟上，我告訴你怎麼走。）
according to　依據、按照

例句

According to your request, we have fixed a bathroom door. That costs USD$200.
根據您的要求，我們修好了浴室門。此花費為美金 200。

Unit 7 報價

E-mail 1

Dear Mr. Yamada

We are very pleased to receive your enquiry of Jan. 28. Please see attached files, ☹ those are the catalog and price list of our products. Also, we are sending you a full range samples, from Nylon 70D to Nylon 1680D in 2 colors (black and white) and 2 coating (PVC and PU). After receiving them, you can examine them. We feel confident that you will agree that our goods are both excellent in quality and very reasonable in price.

From the quotation you will also be able to see that the prices we quoted are very competitive with those similar fabric from the other suppliers, and that all prices are quoted CIF Yokohama, Japan. In addition. We will also be happy to offer you very favorable terms. We can allow an extra 5% discount on an order worth USD$30,000.00 or more.

We would also like to point out that we have been supplying high quality fabric to the Western European and North America markets for many years. All our customers have shown the satisfaction with our products and service. With our experience and expertise, we believe that your turnover will increase sharply soon.

We now look forward to receiving your further instruction in the near future and wish to assure you of our best attention all the times.

Thank you.

Regards/ Cindy

E-mail 1

山田先生您好

我們很高興收到您於一月 **28** 日傳來的詢價單。請見附檔，這些是
目錄及報價單。並且我們也一併將樣品寄出，樣品為尼龍 **70** 丹到
尼龍 **1680** 丹，各有兩種顏色（黑，白），兩種完工膜（**PVC**，
PU）。收到樣品之後，您可細細檢查其品質。您會發現我們的商品
品質優良，價格實惠。

從報價單上，您亦可知道跟其他類似商品的供應商比較起來，我們
的報價十分的實惠。而且報價單上的價格均為 **CIF**（報價已含運費，
保險）橫濱，日本。此外，我們很樂意提供優惠的交易條件：若您
的訂單有超過美元 **30,000.00** 則可得到額外的 **5%** 折扣。

我們高品質的織布外銷西歐跟北美市場多年，客戶對我們的產品跟
服務均十分滿意。藉著我們經驗跟專業幫助，我們希望貴公司的營
業額能快速的成長。

希望很快能收到您進一步的通知，我們保證隨時為貴公司服務。

致上敬意

Cindy

Dialogue

Cindy	Claire, I got reply from Toyo, they said they were very interested in our products.	嘿，Claire。我收到Toyo公司的回信了，他對我們產品有興趣。
Claire	Good, what items they specifically asked?	棒極了！！他們詢問什麼產品？
Cindy	They need all kinds of Nylon fabrics. I have quoted on Nylon fabrics, from 70D to 1680D with 2 colors and 2 coating. Also, the samples were sent accordingly.	他們想要知道尼龍布。我把尼龍布報價給他們，從70D到1680D，各兩色，兩種貼膜都含在報價裡。樣品也一併寄上。
Claire	What's the price term?	價格條件是什麼？
Cindy	CIF Yokohama, Japan. I also offer them 5% discount on an order worth USD$30,000.00 or more. I had discussed this strategy with Joseph. We all agree to offer a competitive price to win the customer first.	CIF 橫濱，日本。而且訂單金額超過美金 USD$30,000.00 就給5%折扣。我跟 Joseph 討論過了，我們同意為了爭取客戶，同意提供更優惠的價格。

抓「龍」TIME

☹ Those are the catalog and price list of our products.

☺ Those are the catalog and quotation of our products.

☹ What items they specific asked?

☺ What items they specific requested?

經典好用句

☺ **have shown the**　表現出……

The soldiers have shown their sincere respect to the President.

戰士們對總統充滿敬意。

☺ **look forward to**　期待 …

look forward to + n. / Ving

We look forward to your reply soon.（加名詞）

We look forward to hearing from you soon.（加動名詞）

我們期待很快收到您的回覆。

字彙精選

■ **coating**　*n*　塗層

The nylon coating is PU, not PVC. You should explain the difference to the customer.

這塊尼龍布的塗層是 PU 不是 PVC，你應該跟客戶解釋兩者的差異。

■ **feel confident**　感到自信，自豪的

We feel very confident about this year's Media Show. It totally catches people's eyes.

對於今年的媒體秀，我們深感信心。這場秀抓住眾人的目光！

■ **excellent**　*adj*　太棒了

Owen's parents are so proud of his performance. it's excellent!! He gets the gold medal.

Owen 的雙親對他表現十分自豪，表演實在太棒了！！他得到了金牌。

■ **favorable**　*adj*　有利的，良好的

Broccoli is proven to be favorable for health. We should have more.

花椰菜被證實了對健康有益，我們應該多吃。

■ **expertise**　*n*　專門的技術，知識

His expertise is astronautics. Only few people can fit in his job.

他的專長技術是航太科學，只有少數人能夠填補他的工作。

■ **turnover**　*n*　營業額

The turnover of SOGO department store in 2014 had increased 25 %.

SOGO 百貨的營業額在 2014 年成長了 25%。

抓龍術大公開

1. Those are the catalog and ~~price list~~ quotation of our products.

這些是目錄及報價單。

報價單

☹price list

☺quotation

"price list"依照字面上的意思為價目表，通常是指生活中一般商家列給顧客看的價格表。然而在國際貿易上，供應商提供價格表給客戶，其價格表的正式名稱為"quotation"，亦稱做報價單。兩者間的不同在於正式的 quotation 報價單，必須詳列交易條件，交期，價格條件等。是一份完整的商品價格資訊。而 price list 通常只列出品項及價格。

例句

We received Goodwin's quotation; their price seems to be very competitive.

我們收到 Goodwin 公司的報價單了，他們的價格看起來滿優惠的。

2. What items they specifically ~~asked~~ requested?

他們詢問什麼產品？

詢問

☹ask

☺request

ask 與 request 的意思相近，ask 通常會是用在 1. 對於一個問題的答覆；2. 不僅僅是一個答案，而可能是食物、方向、幫助等的。而 request 則相近於 ask 的第 2 種用法，且較 ask 更為正式，也比較廣泛地被使用在商業用途上，例如索取目錄"to request a catalogue"。

例句

A: We need 100 meters nylon 420D/PU in black, delivering to Japan before Jan 10.

B: As your request, we will deliver those goods to you before Jan 10.

A：我們需要 100 尼龍 420D/PU 黑色，於 1 月 10 號前送到日本。

B：依照您的要求，我們將會在 1 月 10 號前將這些貨送到日本。

Unit 8 還價

Email

Dear Cindy

It's Yamada Yoji from Toyo Company. Thanks for your quotation of February 16 and the samples of nylon fabric. It's very kind and thoughtful that you sent them all.

We appreciate the good quality of those Nylon samples, but unfortunately your prices appear to be on the high side even for Nylon of this quality. Our customer is with medium-price demand. If we accept your quotation, it would leave us with no profit. As you know, we can't have losing business.

Besides, we regret to inform you that another China supplier has also quoted the same kind of products as you offered. Honestly speaking, the price is only a half of yours. I'm aware of that your quality is better than China products; however, the price difference is so huge that we may use the China manufacturer instead. Your samples are very impressive, and we admire your positive way in handling business. Therefore, we would look forward to cooperating with you. Maybe you can re-check the cost and make more allowance on the quotation.

We hope you can <u>take our order quantity into consideration</u>, during 2014, our company had imported 35x20" containers. Those were nylon only; the polyester and buckle were not included. If our cooperation works, that will be a big order. And I believe that this sales scale will be very considerable for your company.
Look forward to hearing from you soon.
Regards/ Yamada

Cindy 您好
我是 TOYO 公司的山田洋次，謝謝您於 2 月 16 日的報價及樣品。
對於您將樣品全數寄出，我們感到十分感謝。
貴公司所寄來的樣品，品質十分良好。但是以這樣的尼龍布來説，
您的價格實在偏高。如果我們接受貴公司的價格，我公司便沒有任
何利潤。我相信您也認同，沒有人會做賠本生意。
除此之外，不瞞您説，還有另一家中國供應商一樣的商品，報價卻
只有貴公司的一半。我能明白貴公司的品質比中國產品優良。但是
價差實在太大了，以致我們可能會換成中國廠商。
您的樣品實在使我們印象深刻，而且我們很欣賞貴公司正面積極的
商業手法。因此我們很期待雙方能有合作的機會。或許您可重新檢
視您的成本而給我們更多的優惠。
我們亦希望您能將我公司的訂購量也列入考慮因素中。在 2014 年，
我公司就進口了 35 只 20 呎貨櫃。這些數量僅是尼龍布的部分，還
不含聚酯纖維布跟釦具。如果我們可以合作的話，將會是很大的訂
單。我相信這樣的銷售規模對貴公司是十分可觀的。
希望能盡快得到您的回覆
致上敬意
山田

Dialogue

Cindy	Joseph, I got Toyo's reply. <u>As we expected</u>, they bargained over the price.	我收到 TOYO 公司，山田先生的回覆了。如我們所料，他們想要議價。
Joseph	What's the counter-offer?	對方還價多少？
Cindy	They didn't offer me the accurate price. Just hope we can re-check the quotation and offer more competitive one. We think we should make more concession otherwise <u>they won't put the order.</u>	沒有具體的價格。只是希望我們能再檢視報價單，並提供更優惠的價格。我認為我們應該在價格上讓步，不然客戶不會下訂單。
Joseph	Ok, we need to re-work on our cost estimation. What's the freight from Keelung to Yokohama?	好吧，我們先來估算成本。從基隆到橫濱的運費是多少？
Cindy	USD650/20".	一個 20 呎櫃 650 美金。

抓「龍」TIME

☹ We may use the China manufacturer instead.
☺ We may switch to the China manufacturer.
☹ They won't put the order.
☺ They won't place the order.

經典好用句

☺ **take our order quantity into consideration** 將我
們的訂單量列入考慮中

take… into consideration 將……列入考慮中

Stephen picked some countries for his summer vacation;
Japan and China were into consideration. He likes oriental
culture.

夏季旅行 Stephen 選了幾個地點，日本跟中國都列入考慮中。他喜歡
東方文化。

☺ **as we expected** 如我們所料

As we expected, Opera hotel is a very cozy hotel.

如我們所料，Opera 飯店十分溫馨跟舒適。

字彙精選

■ **unfortunately** *adv* 不幸的

After 10 hours flight, Kelly finally arrived the Seattle,
unfortunately, the customer already had left the city.

經過 10 小時的飛行，Kelly 終於抵達西雅圖。不幸的是，客戶已經離開
那裡。

■ **appear to** 似乎是

Fortunately, the car appears to be quite safe. It passed 1,000
times crush test.

幸運的是，這車看起來似乎十分安全。它通過了 **1,000** 次的撞擊實驗。

■ **allowance** *n* 折扣，誤差

The credit card offers 5% allowance on each alcoholic
beverage in the bar.

這張信用卡為酒吧裡每杯酒精飲料提供 **5%** 折扣。

■ **sales scale** *n* 銷售量

Due to the Internet media, the sales scale of record has
become declined.

由於網路媒體的興起，唱片的銷售量開始減少。

■ **counter-offer** 還價

We haven't received the counter offer from Toyo Company.

我們尚未收到 **Toyo** 公司的還價。

■ **accurate** *adj* 精確的

Seiko is famous for its accurate watch around the world.

精工表以其精確的手錶聞名於世。

抓龍術大公開

1. We may ~~use~~ switch to the China manufacturer ~~instead~~.
   我們可能會換成中國廠家。

   更換
   ☹use sth instead
   ☺switch to

   此句中的意思為「換廠商」，**use sth instead** 是有「更換」的意思，但卻不適用於此。可以用 **switch to** 或是 **change to**。

2. They won't ~~put~~ place the order.
   他們不會下訂單。

   下訂單
   ☹put the order
   ☺place the order
   place order　下訂單

   例句
   > Finally, Toyo Company placed their order. The order was 1,000 meter Nylon420D/PU.
   > 最後，Toyo 公司下單了，訂單是 1000 米的 420 丹 PU 塗膜的尼龍布。
   > Please place the order ASAP, we will be off during the Chinese New Year.
   > 請儘快下單，我們將於農曆新年放假。

Part II 文件

Unit 9 還價接受

E-mail 1

Hi, Mr. Yamada

Thanks for your email of Feb 18.

Re: Our price

To comply with your counteroffer, we have pleasure in enclosing our latest quotation which is operative from March 1, 2015. As you can see, we have quoted you our rock-bottom prices, which we hope that you find satisfactory and win the chance of our cooperation.

We hope that our handling of this new quotation will lead to further business between us and mark the beginning of a mutually satisfactory working relationship.

PS

We hereby reiterate that the said offer remains from only for a period of 30 days, and thereafter it will be subject to further confirmation.

We are looking forward to hearing from you

Regards/ Cindy

E-mail 1

尊敬的 Yamada 先生

謝謝您於 2 月 18 的來信

回覆：我方的價格

遵照您的還價，我們欣喜地附上報價單，此價格自 2015 年 3 月 1 日生效。您可從報價單上看到，我們最新報價已經是最低價了，希望貴公司會滿意，藉此開創雙方合作的機會。

藉此新報價單，促成雙方的商業業務往來，並為合作愉快的開端。在此，我們重申，此報價單有效期為 30 天。之後的價格須重新議價。

期待您早日的回覆

致上敬意 / Cindy

Part II 文件

E-mail 2

Hi, Cindy

Thanks for your quotation of Feb 18. We are very satisfied with the new quotation, and would like to place a trial order. We hope that you will supply, and deliver not later than the end of May

Order No. GM2015220

Item

Nylon 420D/PU	Black	3000 m	USD$ 5.75/M
Nylon 420D/PVC	Navy	1000 m	USD$ 5.75/M
Nylon 210D/PU	White	2000 m	USD$ 4.80/M
Nylon 210D/PVC	Rouge	1000m	USD$ 4.80/M

Payment L/C 60 days

We expect to find a good market for these fabric and hope to place further and larger orders with you in the near future.

Please send the PI as the order confirmation.

Thank you.

Regards, Yamada

E-mail 2

嗨 Cindy

謝謝您於 2 月 18 日的報價單，新的報價單我們很滿意，因此先行試單。希望貴公司能於 5 月底前交貨。

訂單號： GM2015220

品項：尼龍布 420D/PU　　黑色　　3000 米　USD$ 5.75/M
　　　尼龍布 420D/PVC　海軍藍 1000 米　USD$ 5.75/M
　　　尼龍布 210D/PU　　白色　　2000 米　USD$ 4.80/M
　　　尼龍布 210D/PVC　紅色　　1000 米　USD$ 4.80/M

付款：信用狀 60 天

希望此批布料能在市場上大受歡迎，期待未來能與貴公司有大量訂單的往來。

請傳訂購確認單

謝謝
山田

Part II 文件

Dialogue

Cindy	Hey, Claire, I finally got the trial order from Toyo's company. I have written so many emails to their sales representative, Mr. Yamada.	嘿，Claire，我終於拿到 Toyo 公司的試單了，我寫了好多電子郵件給他們的業務，山田先生。
Claire	Great! I'm delighted to learn of your achievement in new market development.	我很高興你在開發新市場上，有了成果。
Cindy	Thanks, but the client's payment term is 60 days L/C, I don't think Jose would agree with it. ☹Our company policy is L/C immediately.	謝謝您，但是客戶要求付款條件是信用狀 60 天，我覺得 Jose 不會同意這點。因為公司的政策一向是即期信用狀。
Claire	Let me see.	我看看。
Cindy	☹It's written on the left lower.	他寫在左下角。

抓「龍」TIME

☹ Our company policy is L/C immediately.
☺ Our company policy is L/C at sight.
☹ It's written on the left lower.
☺ It's written on the lower left.

經典好用句

☺ **to comply with** 遵守，順從

The Islamic State doesn't comply with any UN resolution.
伊斯蘭國並不遵守任何聯合國的決議。

☺ **I'm delighted to**… 我很欣喜的

Annie will be delighted to see you; you haven't met since 2005.
Annie 看到你一定很開心，你們從 2005 年後就沒有碰面了。

字彙精選

■ **reiterate** *v* 重申

The China government reiterates its position and policy on Taiwan issue in National People's Congress.
中國政府在人民大會上重申其對台灣議題的立場及政策。

■ **remain** *n/v* 維持，依然

Aden remained silent during the interrogation.
在審問時，Aden 一直保持沉默。

Part II 文件

■ **a period of** 一段時間

We need to do something; the water shortage issue might last for a long period of time.

我們得採取行動，缺水問題可能會持續一段時間。

■ **not later than** 不晚於

常見說法為 no later than，意思相同，但在正式文件上則要用 not later than。

The last part of the goods is to be shipped not later than May, 2015.

最後一批貨必須於 2015 年 5 月前交貨。

■ **payment** *n* 付款

The bank will start to collect the payment next week; you should be ready for that.

銀行下週就開始收帳了，你應該要快點準備。

抓龍術大公開

1. Our company policy is L/C ~~immediately~~ at sight.

公司的政策一向是即期信用狀。

即期信用狀
☹ L/C immediately
☺ L/C at sight

中文裡的即期，在這裡不適用 immediately（馬上地）。在商業用語裡，即期應寫作 at sight

sight 看見，視力

at sight 表示一看到，就是即期的意思

例句

A: What's the payment term of the new client?
B: It's L/C at sight
A：新客戶的付款條件是什麼？
B：即期信用狀。

2. It's written on the ~~left lower~~ lower left.
他寫在左下角。

左下方
☹left lower
☺lower left

一般中文思考裡，我們想說左下方，直覺翻譯過來是 **left lower**…
但在英文裡，要先說上下，再說左右。正確說法應為"**lower left**"。右上
方，應為"**upper right**"。

例句

The boy drew a dinosaur on the paper lower left.
男孩在紙張左下方畫了一只恐龍。

 Unit 10 確認訂單

E-mail 1

Hi, Mr. Yamada

Thanks for your email of Feb 20.

We are glad that through recent emails, we have reached an agreement on the sale of our nylon fabric to Toyo Company; your PO No is GM2015220.

About the payment term, we would like to inform you that according to our company policy, all the L/C should be at sight, not 60 days. Please check our latest quotation, it's written on it. We hope you can understand and accept it.

Our PI No. TO201522 is in duplicate. Please be assured that every contract signed by us will be executed in accordance with our standard export practice. Please read carefully the specification, color, price, terms, and condition etc. If there is any question, please notify at once. If not, please countersign on the P/I and return us one copy by mail for our files.

In order to avoid any possible delay of shipment, we hope you will open L/C upon receipt of this letter. As soon as your L/C arrives in our hand, we will arrange the production, and make sure the shipment will be not

E-mail 1

later than the end of May 2015,
Thank you.
Regards/ Cindy

嗨，山田先生

謝謝您 2 月 20 號的來信。

經過最近的郵件往來，我們很高興我們終於可以達成共識，並出貨尼龍布給貴公司。您的訂單編號 GM2015220

關於付款條件，我們必須通知您，依照我公司規定，所有的信用狀都為即期，而不是 60 天。請您查看最新的報價單，上有明載。希望您諒解。

我方的確認訂單號為 TO201522，一式兩份。請放心，由我方所簽署的每一份合約都將按照標準出口流程執行。請您仔細閱讀規格，顏色，價格，交易條件等。如有任何疑問，請即刻提出。若無疑問，請回簽 PI 並回傳一份給我方留檔。

為避免交期延誤，我方希望在您收到此信時，儘快開信用狀。一旦我方收到信用狀，即刻安排貨物生產，以確保交期不晚於 2015 年 5 月。

謝謝您

E-mail 2

Hi, Cindy

Thank you for your mail and the P/I.

After checking our stock, we found the Nylon stock is not enough. We would like to increase the quantity, and the new order is as following:

Order No GM2015220-1

Item

Nylon 420D/PU	Black	5000 m	USD$ 5.75/M
Nylon 420D/PVC	Navy	2000 m	USD$ 5.75/M
Nylon 210D/PU	White	5000 m	USD$ 4.80/M
Nylon 210D/PVC	Rouge	2000m	USD$ 4.80/M

Payment L/C at sight.

About the payment term, don't worry. L/C at sight is acceptable.

Please revise the P/I, and kindly notice that the goods you deliver us are in every respect equal to the sample.

Thank you.

Regards/ Yamada

E-mail 2

嗨，Cindy

謝謝您的來信跟訂購確認單。

經過清查庫存之後，我們發現我們的尼龍布庫存不足。因此，我方所訂購的數量必須增加，新訂單數量如下

訂單號：GM2015220-1

品項

尼龍布 420D/PU	黑色	5000 米	USD$ 5.75/M
尼龍布 420D/PVC	海軍藍	2000 米	USD$ 5.75/M
尼龍布 210D/PU	白色	5000 米	USD$ 4.80/M
尼龍布 210D/PVC	紅色	2000 米	USD$ 4.80/M

付款：即期信用狀

關於付款條件，不用擔心。我方接受即期信用狀。

請更改訂購確認單，並請注意貴公司所送達的貨物，必須與您所提供的樣品一致。

謝謝

致上敬意 / 山田

Part II 文件

抓「龍」TIME

☹ We hope you will open L/C upon receipt of this letter.
☺ We hope you will issue L/C upon receipt of this letter.
☹ The Nylon stock is not enough.
☺ We don't have enough Nylon stock.

經典好用句

☺ **please be assured**　請放心，我向您保證

Please be assured that Jack will finish his work on time.
請放心，我向您保證 Jack 會及時完成他的工作的。

☺ **in accordance with**　跟……一致

We should make decisions in accordance with the school policy.
我們的決定必須跟學校的政策一致。

字彙精選

■ **duplicate** *adj* 副本，複製

Kelly received a duplicate copy of her loan contract.
Kelly 收到她的貸款合約的副本。

■ **execute** *v* 執行

The military is fully prepared to execute the war mission.
軍隊充分的準備好執行戰爭任務。

■ **notify** *v* 通知

The superior didn't notify us to update the computer system.
公司上級並未通知我們要更新電腦系統。

■ **at once** *adv* 即刻，馬上，一起

Owen went back to school at once to get this homework.
Owen 馬上回學校去拿他的作業。

■ **countersign** *v/n* 會簽，簽名

Please countersign on this contract, or it will not be valid.
請在合約上會簽，否則合約無法生效。

■ **revise** *v* 修改

The teachers work together to revise the school curriculum.
老師們合力修改學校課程。

Part II 文件

抓龍術大公開

1. We hope you will ~~open~~ issue L/C upon receipt of this letter.

   我方希望在您收到此信時，儘快開信用狀。

   開信用狀
   ☹open L/C
   ☺issue L/C

   一般請客戶開信用狀，常見誤用 open L/C，正確用法為 issue。

   例句

   > We have arranged the items are in production, please issue L/C ASAP.
   >
   > 我們已經安排貨物生產了，請儘快開信用狀。

2. ~~The Nylon stock is not enough.~~ We don't have enough nylon stock.

   我們的尼龍布庫存不足。

   在說某某東西庫存量不夠時，不能以此物當主詞。
   正確說法應為
   There is not enough Nylon stock. 或
   We don't have enough Nylon stock.

Unit 11 包裝

Hi, Mr. Yamada

<u>Shipment Notice</u>

We are very pleased to inform you that the order no. GM2015220-1 is ready for shipment. The detail is as follows

Item

Nylon 420D/PU	Black	5000 m	/50m x 100 rolls
Nylon 420D/PVC	Navy	2000 m	/50m x 40 rolls
Nylon 210D/PU	White	5000 m	/50m x 100 rolls
Nylon 210D/PVC	Rouge	2000m	/50m x 40 rolls

S/O : 5287

ETD : 25 April, 2015 Keelung, Taiwan

ETA : 10 May , 2015 Yokohama, Japan

Please see the attached files, those are the invoice and packing list of the shipment. If there is anything not clear, please feel free to contact me.

Thank you

Regards/ Cindy

E-mail 1

尊敬的山田先生

<u>出貨通知</u>

我們很榮幸通知您，關於訂單 GM20152220-1 已經生產完成，準備出貨，細節如下：

項目

尼龍布 420D/PU	黑色	5000 米 /50 米 x 100 支
尼龍布 420D/PVC	深藍色	2000 米 /50 米 x 40 支
尼龍布 210D/PU	白色	5000 米 /50 米 x 100 支
尼龍布 210D/PVC	紅色	2000 米 /50 米 x 40 支

艙單號：5287

預計出發日： 四月 25 日，2015 基隆，台灣

預計抵達日：五月 10 日，2015 橫濱，日本

附件為發票及包裝明細，若有任何問題，請與我聯絡。

謝謝

Cindy 敬上

Part II 文件

E-mail 2

Hi, Cindy

We received the shipment notice, thank you.

However, after reading the packing list, we found out there is no shipping mark on our goods. That's a very critical problem; it will cause a serious trouble for our company. Each roll should have a shipping mark on itself.

Let me know if shipping mark is arranged as we requested.

Regards/ Yamada

E-mail 2

Hi, Cindy

我收到裝運通知了，謝謝。

但是，看過包裝明細之後，我們發現貴公司在貨物上並沒有貼上麥頭。這是一個十分嚴重的問題，會給我司製造麻煩。在每捲貨物上，都必須要有麥頭。

我司必須知道貴公司是否有按我方要求製作麥頭。

山田敬上

Dialogue

Cindy	Claire, we need to open a meeting. There is a serious problem	Claire，我們需要開個會，有麻煩了。
Claire	Ok, what's the matter?	好的，什麼事情？
Cindy	I was negligent in Toyo shipping mark; all the goods is without shipping mark.	因為我的疏忽，Toyo 的麥頭沒做。現在出貨了，麥頭全沒貼。
Claire	What? Where are those goods now?	怎麼會這樣？現在貨在哪裡？
Cindy	The container is on its way to the container yard.	正在去貨櫃場的路上。
Claire	You call the driver and ask him to return to our factory now. Unload those goods, and get the shipping mark ready. We have to get things done in an hour.	妳打電話給司機，叫他開回來。將貨卸下，把麥頭準備好，我們必須在 1 小時內完成此事。
Cindy	But there will be an extra cost for the container tractor. It's so humiliating. How I can make such a stupid mistake.	但是，這樣會有多一筆拖車費，真是太糟糕了，我怎麼會犯這樣蠢的錯誤。

| Claire | You <u>had your lesson in a hard way</u>; don't feel remorse. To fix the mistake is the first priority. Without shipping mark, all the goods will be rejected by Japan Customs. | 記取教訓，不要再自責了。優先把問題處理好才是重點。沒有麥頭，貨到日本海關會全數被退回。 |

抓「龍」TIME

☹ The detail is as below.
☺ The detail is as follows.
☹ We need to open a meeting.
☺ We need to call a meeting.

經典好用句

☺ **get things done**　把事搞定

Before taking long vacation, you should get things done.
在放長假之前，你得先把事情搞定。

☺ **had one's lesson in hard way**　你學到了教訓

A: Adam was arrested for drunk driving last weekend.
B: I hope he had his lesson in hard way.
A：Adam 上週末因為酒駕被捕
B：我希望他能學到教訓。

字彙精選

■**tractor** *n* 牽引機

Container tractor 貨櫃拖車

There were many container tractors on the highway. The traffic was a mess.

高速公路上都是貨櫃拖車，交通一團亂。

■**negligent** *adj* 粗心的，疏忽的

A negligent mother left her baby in the car alone.

一個粗心的媽媽將小寶寶單獨留在車上。

■**humiliating** *adj* 丟臉的

It's so humiliating; the tourist took a leak in public.

好丟臉哦，那觀光客在公共場所小便。

■**remorse** *n* 悔恨，自責

Adam was full of remorse because of drunk driving

Adam 對於酒駕而自責不已。

■**priority** *n* 優先權

Being a mother is her first priority, so she resigned from her job last month.

當個好媽媽是她最重要的事，所以她上個月辭職了。

■**reject** *v* 拒絕

Adam was rejected by Kelly; she doesn't want to go out with him.

Adam 被 Kelly 拒絕了，她不想和他出門。

抓龍術大公開

1. The detail is as ~~below~~ follows.

細節如下。

如下

☹as below

☺as follows

若要用 below，則為"For the details, please see below."。as 後面應該是接 follows。

例句

The detail is as follows, please read it carefully.

細節如下，請仔細閱讀。

2. We need to ~~open~~ call a meeting.

我們需要開個會。

開會

☹open a meeting

☺call a meeting

也可以說是"We need to hold a meeting."。

例句

We need to hold a meeting, there will be a special client coming to our office tomorrow.

我們得開會，明天有位特別的客戶到公司來訪。

Unit 12 出貨

E-mail 1

Hi, Yamada

Thanks for your prompt reply.

<u>Shipping Mark</u>

Thanks for the reminder; we had towed the container back to our warehouse and had the shipping mark on each roll. Please see the attached file. These are our shipping goods, and you can see the shipping mark is on each roll as your request.

We apologize for the trouble and confusion we caused and ensure that <u>this mistake won't never happen again.</u>

The shipping document will be ready this Friday; we will send the original document to our bank for negotiation and the copy document to you by DHL. The document will be

Invoice

Packing list

B/L

Insurance policy

Certificate of original

Please note

E-mail 1

The shipping sample will be enclosed with the document by DHL
If there is any question, please let me know.
Regards/ Cindy

尊敬的山田先生

謝謝您即時的回覆

<u>麥頭</u>

謝謝您的提醒，我們將貨櫃拖回倉庫，並且在每捲布料上貼上麥頭。請見附檔，這是出貨時的照片。從照片裡，您可以看到每捲布上依照您的要求都有麥頭。

對於所造成的混亂，我們深感抱歉。並在此向您保證，類似的情況不會再發生。

出貨文件本週五會準備好，正本文件會送銀行押匯。附本會以 **DHL** 快遞給您。我方所提供的文件為

發票

包裝明細

提單

保單

產地證明

請留意：出貨樣會同文件一併以ＤＨＬ寄出

若有任何不清楚的地方，請您提出。

Cindy 敬上

E-mail 2

Hi,Cindy

Thanks for your reply.

We are pleased to know that all the shipping mark has arranged. Please make sure that this mistake won't happen again. Goods without the shipping mark are forbidden for Japan Customs, and it could result in a serious problem for our company.

We need your guarantee on this issue.

Thank you

Regards/ Yamada

Cindy

謝謝您的回覆

我們很慶幸所有的貨都貼上麥頭了。請務必確認類似的情況不會再發生。日本海關嚴禁沒有麥頭的貨物進口,而且會導致我公司嚴重的後果。

我司需要貴公司在此議題上承諾。

謝謝

山田敬上。

Joseph	How was the shipment of Toyo's first order?	Toyo 公司的第一次出貨還順利嗎？
Cindy	We had an unexpected incident yesterday; I missed the shipping mark. After discussing with Claire, we towed the container back, and placed the shipping mark. We were lucky we still caught up with the closing date.	昨天有些突發狀況，我漏做了麥頭。跟 Claire 討論之後，我們決定將貨櫃拖回來。將麥頭貼上。很幸運的，我們還是有趕上結關。
Joseph	<u>That's close</u>. I'm glad that the problem was solved by your team work. Remember, fixing the mistake is the priority, don't be afraid of admitting mistakes. Anything happen, you can always come to me or Claire. <u>We are behind you.</u>	很驚險吶。我很高興看到你們透過團隊合作解決了問題。記住，不要害怕承認錯誤，我們必須要馬上改正錯誤。有事情，隨時來找我或是 Claire。我們是你的後盾。
Cindy	I really appreciate that.	真的很感激。
Joseph	☹ <u>You are welcome.</u> We are a team.	不客氣。

抓「龍」TIME

☹ This mistake won't never happen again.
☺ This mistake won't happen again.
☹ You are welcome.
☺ No problem.

經典好用句

☺ **that's close**　好驚險

That's close. We almost miss the fight.
好險，我們差點趕不上飛機了

☺ **we are behind you**　我們支持你

A: I'm so nervous about tomorrow's interview.
B: Relax, we are behind you.
A: 明天要面試了，我好緊張。
B: 放輕鬆，我們都支持你。

字彙精選

■ **apologize**　*v*　道歉

The woman finally apologized to the public; however, it's too late.
那位女士終於向大眾道歉，然而已經太遲了。

■ **confusion**　*n*　混亂

There was confusion when the earthquake rattled. Everyone was panic.
發生地震時，一片混亂。大家都十分慌張。

■ **forbidden** *adj* 禁止的

Drunk driving is forbidden in many countries. It's a felony

酒駕在許多國家都是禁止的，這是項重罪。

■ **result in** 導致

High temperatures also result in highly power consumption.

高溫亦導致用電量高。

■ **guarantee** *n/v* 保證

The supplier guaranteed that we can get the new iPhone 6 next week.

供應商保證我們下週能拿到新的 iPhone6。

■ **incident** *n* 事件

The restaurant blackout incident brought the total number of injured people to 17.

餐廳停電事件導致 17 人受傷。

抓龍術大公開

1. This mistake won't ~~never~~ happen again.

這樣的錯誤不會再發生。

不會再發生

☹ won't never happen again

☺ won't happen again

這裡的 **never** 是多餘的，

正確用法

won't happen again.

例句

A: I'm sorry for the mistake.

B: Don't apologize; make sure it won't happen again.

A：很抱歉發生這樣的錯誤。

B：用不著道歉。下次別再發生就好。

2. ~~You are welcome.~~ No problem.

不用客氣。

在一般對話中，回應對方的「謝謝」，接的是「不用客氣」"You are welcome."無誤。但是在此情境對話則不適合。兩人為熟識的同事，在討論問題後，一般不會用 You are welcome. 這樣生疏的回應方式。You are welcome 比較適用於不熟的兩人，一方表示謝意說的。如問路的時候。

在此情境對話中，Joseph 的不客氣正確說法可以是"No problem!"，"Not a problem!"，"Anytime!"或是"Sure thing."等說法。小心！不要因為過份的客氣，而造成與同事之間的生疏感喔！

例句

A: Hey, thanks for watching my kids when I was not around.

B: Sure thing.

A：謝謝你在我出門時幫我看小孩。

B：沒問題。

Part III
人際
Relationship

Unit 1 拜訪同事

In the office
在辦公室

Ivan	Finally, all the work is done. It's late, let's <u>call it a day</u>. Jack, Gabriel, do you like to have dinner in my place? My wife is not at home. We can order some takeout.	終於工作都完成了，已經很晚了。該休息了。Jack，Gabriel，要不要來我家吃飯，我太太不在。我們可以叫點外賣。
Gabriel	Sure! Jack and I would love to. We are hungry.	好哇，Jack 跟我都沒問題，也餓了。

In Ivan's house
在Ivan家

Ivan	What do you like to eat?	你們要吃什麼？
Gabriel	Pizza and some fried chicken. Thank you.	披薩跟炸雞，謝謝你。

Jack	Ivan, you have a really beautiful house there.	Ivan，你家很漂亮。
Ivan	Thanks. My wife spent a lot of time on the decoration. She read Elle Decoration, Metropolitan Home, and even hired an interior designer for that. Can you believe that? After 2 months, we will have an exquisite bathroom and many storage cabinets.	謝謝，我太太花了很多時間裝潢。她看了 Elle Decoration，Metropolitan Home 雜誌，然後還請了室內設計師。你能相信嗎？再過兩個月，我們將會有個很精緻的浴室跟許多的儲存櫃。
Jack	Of course.	我相信。
Gabriel	Hey, it's a family photo. Your daughter is very adorable; she has your eyes, how old is she?	這是全家福照耶，你女兒真的好可愛，她眼睛像你，她幾歲了？
Ivan	Just 5, she is my angel but can be a handful sometimes. My wife always says that I spoil her.	五歲了。她很可愛但是有時候很難管得動。我太太總說我寵壞她了。
Jack	Plan to have another one?	還想生一個嗎？

Part III 人際

Ivan	Not really, we already have our hands full with this one. She is enough for me. Besides, my work has occupied most of my time, and I travel a lot. I feel sorry that I wasn't around all the time.	沒有耶，這一個就讓我們忙不過來，一個就夠了。而且，我工作占據我太多時間，我又常出差。我對家人感到很抱歉因為不能常在家。
Gabriel	Dude, have you heard about the rumor? Adam is resigning his job.	嘿，老兄，有聽到謠言嗎？Adam 要離職了。
Ivan	Really? I don't know that. It's kind of weird. I haven't heard of anything.	真的？我不知道。有點奇怪，我沒聽到什麼風聲。
Gabriel	He wants to keep it quiet. Therefore, only few people know it.	他想要保持低調，所以沒有幾個人知道。
Jack	Did he tell you the reason?	他有告訴你原因嗎？
Gabriel	I overheard that he has some family problems. He tried to persuade his wife, but was in vain. His wife gave him an ultimatum, and left him no choice.	我不小心聽到好像是家庭問題。他試著想要說服他太太但是沒有用。他太太給他最後通牒，讓他無從選擇。

| Ivan | That's a pity. I get along pretty well with him. I know he has ambitions on this job, and the boss values his performance a lot. | 好可惜，我們處得還不錯。我知道他對工作野心勃勃，老闆也看中他的表現。 |

抓「龍」TIME

☹ Adam is resigning his job.
☺ Adam is resigning from his job.

經典好用句

☺ **call it a day**　今天就到這吧

Let's call it a day. I'd like to go home and have some rest.
今天就到這吧，我想回去休息了。

☺ **keep it quiet**　保持低調

Carl dropped out of school; his parents like to keep it quiet.
Carl 退學了，他們父母不想張揚此事。

Part III 人際

字彙精選

■ **exquisite** *adj* 精緻的，講究的

Even though the exquisite doll house is so expensive, Eric bought it for his daughter.

儘管那精緻的娃娃屋十分昂貴，Eric 還是為他女兒買下了。

■ **cabinet** *n* 儲藏櫃

You should not buy anything. Our food cabinets are already full.

你不要再買東西了。我們的食物儲藏櫃已經滿了。

■ **adorable** *adj* 可愛的

Judith is so adorable, and everyone loves her.

Judith 好可愛，大家都喜歡她。

■ **hands full** 忙不過來

Glen has his hands full with his estate business.

Glen 為了他的地產事業忙得不可開交。

■ **occupy** *v* 占據，使用

You have to wait. The restroom is occupied.

洗手間有人。你得等等。

■ **ultimatum** *n* 最後通牒

The teacher issued an ultimatum to the students. If they don't submit the report, they will be flunked out.

老師給學生下最後通牒，如果報告再不交就會被當掉。

抓龍術大公開

1. Adam is resigning from his job.
Adam要離職了。

離職
☹resign his job.
☺resign from his job.

resign 的意思為辭職，通常只要用 resign 就能完全地表達要辭去工作的意思，所以在句尾不加 his job。而如果要強調從 job（工作上）或是 position（職位上）辭職，那就要加 from，例如："resign from his job"；"resign from this position" 等用法。
除了 resign 之外，辭職還可以用 quit，然而 quit 和 resign 這兩者在用法上有些許程度上的差異。quit 這單字，當放棄，或是離職。因此當我們想要說離職時，首先想到便是此字。但是 I quit!! 是帶有不幹了，說走就走的意思。一般會被認為是在離職程序上較不完整，時間較短，或是並沒有得到正式的同意。而 resign，則被認為是有按一般程序，跟主管報備，做好職務交接再離職。

Part III 人際

 Unit 2 接機

In the office
在辦公室

Jack	Gabriel, Henk will be arriving in Taiwan this afternoon. You and I are going to pick him up and help him to settle down. Did you book the hotel?	Gabriel，Henk 下午就到台灣。我們去接機，幫他安頓好，飯店訂好了嗎？
Gabriel	Yep, the Yoho Taipei. It's booked under his name. Will Ivan go with us?	訂好 Yoho Taipei 飯店了，登記在他名下。Ivan 跟我們一起去嗎？
Jack	No, he can't. He has a meeting with VP. We'd better be on the way soon. One more thing, you know our dress code is pretty casual here. But, it's important to look professional when a client is visiting and we should pay attention to details.	他沒辦法，副總找他開會。我們最好要出發了。有件事，你知道我們公司對員工穿著沒有什麼規定。不過，當跟客戶來訪時，最好能夠注意細節，讓自己看起來更專業。

| Gabriel | I understand, and I'll have my business suit and tie on when we meet Henk. Will he visit our office today? | 了解，等等跟 Henk 碰面時我會把西裝穿好，領帶打好。今天 Henk 會進我們公司嗎？ |
| Jack | I don't know. He probably will have jet lag. Maybe we should take him right to the hotel then, so he can have some sleep. | 我不知道，或許他會有時差。或許他想要回飯店好好休息睡覺。 |

In the Airport
在機場

Jack	Hi, Henk, welcome to Taiwan. It's been a long time. How was the flight?	Hi，Henk，歡迎來台灣。好久不見，一路都好嗎？
Henk	Jack! Good to see you. <u>You look great</u>, and <u>you are skinny.</u> Well, this one was uneventful, except for a little turbulence. But I did get a good sleep on the plane, even the baby next me was crying all the way.	Jack，真高興看到你，你看起來不錯嘛。你瘦了。旅程還算順利，除了偶爾有些小氣流。不過我倒是睡的很好，即使隔壁的小孩一直哭也沒影響我。
Jack	Glad to hear that. It's my coworker, Gabriel.	不錯，這位是我同事，Gabriel。

Hank	It's nice to meet you, Gabriel, just call me Henk. I'm not big on formalities. 🙁 I'm an easy person.	很 榮 幸 見 到 你，Gabriel，叫我 Henk 就好，我比較不拘小節，容易相處。
Gabriel	Nice to meet you, Henk.	很 高 興 見 到 你，Henk。
Jack	Henk, would you like to have an informal dinner with us tonight, Just Ivan, Gabriel and me, only 3 of us. I'd like to have a small reception for you. Ivan was expectedly tied up this afternoon. He is very eager to meet you.	Henk， 晚 上， 我、Gabriel、Ivan 三個人有個小聚餐，只有我們三人，想幫你接風。你要不要來呢？Ivan 下午剛好有個會走不開，他很想跟你碰面。
Hank	Sure! I would love to. If you don't mind, can you take me to the hotel before the dinner? I need to freshen up.	當 然， 我 很 樂 意。 可是，可以先載我回飯店嗎？我需要梳洗一番。

抓「龍」TIME

🙁 You are skinny.
☺ You are slim.
🙁 I'm an easy person.
☺ I am an easy-going person.

經典好用句

☺ **You look great!** 你看起來不錯嘛

A: It's been a long time, you look great.

B: I have been jogging for 4 months; my doctor said that I should have more exercise.

A：好久不見，你看起來不錯啊

B：我開始慢跑 4 個月了，我醫生建議我要多運動。

☺ **if you don't mind** 如果你不介意的話

If you don't mind, I would like to leave work early today. I have an appointment with my dentist.

如果你不介意的話，我今天會提早下班，我跟牙醫有約。

字彙精選

■ **uneventful** *adj* 沒什麼特別的，平靜的

Although Alison just got her driver license, the car was running perfectly and the journey was very uneventful.

雖然 Alison 剛拿到駕照，但是車子開得很順，旅程一切平靜。

■ **turbulence** *n* 亂流

Jason experienced severe turbulence during last flight, so he would not take plane anymore.

Jason 上次搭機時遇到了強烈的亂流，所以他再也不搭飛機了。

Part III 入境

■**formalities** *n* formality的複數；形式，俗套

With the progress of the times, some Chinese wedding formalities have been cancelled.

隨著時代的進步，一些中國婚禮的俗套都已經取消了。

■**informal** *adj* 非正式的

The mayor made an informal speech to stress out his position.

市長發表了一場非正式的演說來重申自己的立場。

■**reception** *n* 歡迎會

A reception will be held this afternoon. You should dress up.

下午有場歡迎會，你應該打扮打扮。

■**eager** *adj* 想要

The company is eager to expand into new markets.

這家公司很急著想要擴展新的市場。

抓龍術大公開

1. You are ~~skinny~~ slim.

你很瘦。

在形容胖瘦的時候，我們常會直覺地想到 fat and thin，但其實在形容人的身材的胖、瘦上並不只有這樣的說法。也跟中文裡會以豐腴、勻稱等的形容詞來形容身材的方式一樣，有「褒」也有「貶」。例如以 fat 形容身材，多帶有貶義，如能用 plump（豐滿的）形容女子，stout（壯碩的）形容男子，相對起來就好聽多了。

用來形容「瘦」的說法有很多種，最常聽到的有 slender、slim、thin、

skinny 等，其中以 slender、slim 是形容身材修長、苗條，thin 則介於褒貶之間，而 skinny 則有皮包骨的感覺。由對話中，我們得知 Henk 應是在稱讚 Jack 瘦身有成，所以應該説 slim 或是 slender 最為恰當。

例句

You are skinny, you should eat more.
你太瘦了，要多吃一點。
She's blonde and slender.
她有一頭金髮及修長勻稱的身材。

2. I'm an easy-going person.
我很隨和。

隨和
☹ easy
☺ easy-going

若單用 easy，會比較像是「我是個很隨便的人」。在説我是一個隨和的人時，除了用 easy-going 之外，還可以説"I am easy to deal with."。

例句

Adam is an easy-going person. He is very friendly.
Adam 為人隨和，他對人很友善。

Part III 人際

 Unit 3 客戶來訪

Dialogue

Jack	May I have your attention, please. I'd like to take a moment to express my sincere thanks to Henk for his great efforts. As you know, our company and Vasa have reached an agreement to distribute our earphone in Sweden. This joint venture is worth celebrating because it marks our entry into the Sweden digital accessories market.	請各位注意，我想要藉此機會表達我對 Henk 的誠摯謝意。各位都知道，我們公司跟 Vasa 達成了在瑞典的耳機銷售合約。我們在此慶祝我們的產品進入瑞典的電子配件市場。
Henk	Thanks, Jack, the pleasure is mine. I'm glad to be here today.	謝謝，Jack，我今天很高興能在此，是我的榮幸。

Ivan	With Vasa's well-established distribution network in Sweden, we can both stay one step ahead of the competition. On behalf of my coworkers and myself, I am glad to say that Inno is delighted to work with an industry leader like Vasa. I can foresee the huge growth for both of our companies over the next few years.	因為 Vasa 在瑞典完善的銷售網，我們雙方都能領先競爭者。我僅代表我與我的同事們，很榮幸能與 Vasa 合作。也能預測到在未來的幾年，我們雙方的業績將會迅速成長。
Henk	You two are too modest. Without your smart products, there is no possibility for our cooperation.	你們兩位實在太客氣了。沒有好的產品，就不會這次的合作。
Jack	You have a way of always hitting the nail on the head. Henk, how long are you going to stay in Taipei? Are there any places you'd like to see while you are here? I'd be happy to show you around.	你總是有辦法講到重點。對了，你這次打算在台北停留幾天？有什麼想去的地方嗎？我可以帶你去轉轉。

Part III 人際

Henk	I'd like to see Taipei 101; I heard it's a beautiful building. I will be tied up in meetings; but still want to <u>mix business with pleasure</u> on this trip. After all, I'm in Asia.	聽說台北 101 是個很漂亮的建築物,我想去看看。雖然會議很多,但是我還是想在閒暇之餘去看看。畢竟,難得到了亞洲。
Jack	Don't worry; we will try to shorten the meeting. By the way, Is Tiw in Taipei? He lined me last week, and mentioned that he would go to China directly without stopping by Taipei.	別擔心,我們會把會議縮短的。對了,Tiw 在台北嗎?他上週 line 我,說他直接去中國沒有停台北。
Henk	That's right. He is so fascinated with old Chinese architecture; I bet he is in Zhou Zhuang now. He's gonna stay there for couple days. Then next week, I'll fly to Beijing to join him. We will go to the Great Wall together.	沒錯。他真的好喜歡中國的傳統建築,我猜他現在應該在周莊。他會在那裡停留幾天,下週我再飛去北京跟他碰面,我們一起去長城。
Jack	Sounds like you have a great plan.	聽起來你們都計畫好了。

| Henk | Just do my best. | 盡量做好該做的。 |

抓「龍」TIME

☹ Are there any places you'd like to see?
☺ Are there any sights you'd like to see?

經典好用句

☺ **hit the nail on the head** 一針見血，說得很中肯

You just hit the nail on the head with the comment about her; she is truly a selfish girl.

你對她的評語真是一針見血，她真的是個自私的女生。

☺ **mix business with pleasure** 工作之餘兼觀光

My boss is very mad at Adam; he mixed business with pleasure on the business trip in Korea.

老闆對 Adam 很生氣，他去韓國出差時還有心情觀光。

Part III 人際

字彙精選

■ **sincere** *adj* 誠摯的

Please accept my sincere apology. I didn't mean to say such bad words.

請接受我誠摯的道歉，我不是故意說出那些傷人的話。

■ **joint venture** *n* 合資企業

As a sales manager of a joint venture, Russell has to travel a lot.

作為一個合資企業的業務經理，Russell 必須常常出差。

■ **distribution** *n* 分配

Due to the unfair distribution of inheritance, the siblings sued each other.

因為遺產的分配不公，兄弟姐妹相互提告。

■ **foresee** *v* 預測

Nobody can foresee what will happen in the future.

沒有人能預測到未來會發生什麼事。

■ **tied up** 綁住

Rick will come back soon. He is tied up in an important meeting now.

Rick 快就會回來了。他現在正在有個重要的會議走不開。

■ **shorten** *v* 縮短

The new labor policy could shorten the working hours of workers.

新的勞工法會縮短勞工工時。

抓龍術大公開

1. Are there any ~~places~~ sights you'd like to see?
有什麼想去的地方嗎？

在情境對話中，Jack 想問的是 Hank 想不想去一些觀光景點看看。句尾用的是 to see，所以應寫成"Are there any sights you'd like to see?"。如果要説 place 的話，則應該説成"Are there any places you'd like to go?"。

一般用以表達景點，我們會説 sights，例如觀光就是 sightseeing。

例句

They had visited lots sights of Stockholm.
他們拜訪了斯德哥爾摩許多景點。

Unit 4 面試

Dialogue

Webber	Meredith, how would you describe your character?	Meredith，説説妳自己的個性。
Meredith	I'm a tenacious, adventurous person. I would say I thrive on adversity.	我是個堅毅，有冒險精神的人，能越挫越勇。
Webber	Ok, why do you want to be a sales representative of the Grey Product?	好的，請問妳為什麼想要成為 Grey 的業務代表？
Meredith	Well, I grew up with my grandparents. I care about the old people. However, I'm not smart enough to be a doctor. Therefore, I would try another way. To work in the medical equipment business can make me feel that I'm able to help patients.	是這樣的，我從小跟我祖父母一起生活。我關心老年人，但是我又不夠聰明，當不了醫生。因此，我試著其他方向，醫療器材事業讓我覺得我可以幫助病人。

	As I know, the Grey Product is the leading manufacturer in the medical equipment field.	就我所知，Grey 一直是醫療用品產業的領先者。
Webber	☹ Interesting idea. Besides your passion, what's your initial idea about the medical equipment industry?	很有意思的想法。除了妳的熱情之外，妳對醫療器材產業有什麼了解？
Meredith	First, it's a challenging and extremely rewarding work. Second, it's a high technology and precise industry. We must constantly adapt and innovate to ensure success in a growing market.	首先，這份工作充滿挑戰，待遇也相對不錯。第二，這是一項高科技跟精密的產業。我們必須不斷地創新跟改良，才能在市場佔有一席之地。
Webber	I'm glad that you did the work. Yes, Indeed. As you know, we are an international company, in your opinion, what is the most important thing when communicating with people from other countries?	很高興你有做了研究，妳說得沒錯。如妳所知，我們是國際企業，妳認為在跟國外客戶溝通時，最重要的是什麼？

Part III 人際

Meredith	I will always get myself fully prepared with the relevant data and researches, and then spend some time understanding their cultural background. It's quite important. For those who are not native speakers of English, the cultural differences are sometimes reflected in spoken or written English. To understand what your customers say or write, you have to understand their cultures first.	我會把相關的資料，研究都準備好。然後花點時間去了解他們的文化背景。這件事很重要，因為就母語不是英語的人士而言，文化的差異常常會反映在英文說、寫上。要了解客戶所說的或是寫的，就必須先懂他們的文化。
Webber	Can you make some examples?	妳可以舉例嗎？
Meredith	Sure. Weeks ago, my Egypt customer called me; he kept telling me "I eyes your fax". At the beginning, I was so confused. It took me a while to realize that he was saying "I saw your fax".	當然。幾個星期前，我一位埃及客戶打電話給我，電話裡，他一直說 "I eyes your fax"。起初，我根本聽不懂。後來花了好大功夫，我才知道他說的是我看到你的傳真了。

| Webber | It looks like you are the perfect candidate for this job. But we have to interview with all the candidates today. We'll let you know the result tomorrow. | 看來，妳是此份工作的不二人選。但是，我們還是要面試完今天所有的求職者。明天就會通知你結果。 |
| Meredith | I am looking forward to hearing from you and seeing you again. | 期待能再與貴公司聯絡，再見。 |

抓「龍」TIME

☹ I care about the old people.
☺ I care about the elderly.
☹ Interesting idea.
☺ Interesting thought.

經典好用句

☺ **thrive on adversity**　越挫越勇

Happy people thrive on adversity; they always see the bright side.

快樂的人越挫越勇，他們總是處處往好處想。

Part III 人際

字彙精選

■ **tenacious** *adj* 堅毅的

Sandra is a tenacious lady; she wouldn't give up easily.
Sandra 是個堅毅的女性,她不會輕言放棄。

■ **initial** *adj* 最初的

The initial problem has been solved; the homeless got their shelters.
最基本的問題已經解決,流浪漢有了棲身之處。

■ **extremely** *adv* 非常的,極端的

He is a marvelous employee, who works extremely hard.
他是一個超棒的職員,工作非常努力。

■ **precise** *adj* 精密的

The connector has a precise design. The competitor can't imitate it.
這連接器的設計十分精密,競爭者無法模仿。

■ **constantly** *adv* 不斷的

Derek is constantly checking his patient. He is a good doctor.
Derek 不斷地查看他病人的狀況,他是個好醫生。

■ **innovate** *v* 改革,創新

The government must innovate in order to make a progress for our country.
政府必須改革,我們國家才會進步。

抓龍術大公開

1. I care about the elderly.

我關心老年人。

老年人

☹the old people

☺the elderly

用英文説「老人家」時，"**the old people**"雖然在字面上意義雖然無誤，但是其實有更好的説法 **the elderly**，更為正式也較不失禮，所以建議大家避免使用 **the old people**。在這裡要注意的是，**the elderly** 也可以説是 **the elderly people**。

例句

There are a lot elderly people living in this village.

這村莊住了許多老人家。

2. Interesting ~~idea~~ thought.

很有意思的想法。

想法

☹idea

☺thought

idea 與 thought 在中文的意思中相近，但在英文裡的用法卻不太相同。idea 一般指的是能解決某件事的方式、意見或是作法。而 thought 指的是對某件事的想法，或是概念。而依照對話當中的內容，在這裡應該説是 interesting thought 而非 interesting idea。

例句

I have an idea. We can order takeout tonight.

我有個主意，我們今晚叫外賣。

I don't have any thought on that problem.

關於那個問題，我沒有什麼看法。

Unit 5 帶新同事

Dialogue

| Webber | Meredith, welcome to the Grey Product, it's nice to have you join us. | Meredith，歡迎妳來。很高興妳能加入我們公司。 |
| Meredith | Thank you. Mr. Webber. It's a new chapter in my career, I've been dreaming about working in the Grey Product. Now, here I am. I'm ready for all the new challenges and opportunities…, and the most important is, the new colleague. | 謝謝您，Webber。這是我職場全新的一頁，我一直夢想能來 Grey Product 公司上班。現在，我如願了。準備好面對所有的挑戰跟機會。當然，最重要的是 - 新同事。 |

Webber	I'm sure you can get along well with our co-workers. They are a bunch of nice people. You will find that we have more flexibility here, but there are still some formal rules you need to follow. First, I want to fill you in with some informal dos and don'ts.	我想妳跟我們同事相處一定沒有問題，他們是一群好人。我們這裡的規矩並不嚴。但是仍有些正式的規矩妳需要遵守。首先，我先告訴妳一些不成文的可做，不可做的事。
Meredith	I'm all ears.	我洗耳恭聽。
Webber	Well, we don't need to punch in and out here. But since we are on an honor system for filling out time sheets, we hope everyone arrives on time and doesn't leave early without a good reason.	我們不需要打卡，上下班時間是榮譽制的，自填表格。但是我們還是希望員工能準時上班，沒有什麼重要的事不要早退。
Meredith	That sounds reasonable.	聽起來很合理。

Part III 人際

Webber	And of course, we don't mind personal phone calls and emails. But we don't hope everyone spend much time on checking the smart phone. You know what I mean.	當然,員工可以打私人電話或是收個人郵件。但是我們希望員工不要花時間在滑手機上面。妳知道我的意思的。
Meredith	Sure, no problem.	當然,這沒問題。
April	Hi, Webber, why are you here?	Hi,Webber,你為什麼在這裡?
Webber	Hi, April, it's our new sales representative, Meredith. Meredith, this is April, our accountant. I'm just showing Meredith around.	Hi,April,這是我們的新業務 Meredith,Meredith,這是我們的會計,April。我正帶 Meredith 到處看看。
April	Hi, Meredith. Webber, may I have a word with you? If you don't mind, I can take Meredith. Your face looks not good, you should take some rest.	Hi,Meredith。Webber,借一步說話。如果你不介意的話,我可以帶 Meredith。你臉色看起來不太好,你應該去休息。

April	Meredith, I'll show you around. Any question about our company?	Meredith，我帶妳到處看看。對我們公司有什麼要問的嗎？
Meredith	Actually, I do. Just girls' talk, Are there some subjects that we shouldn't talk about?	事實上，有。就當是女生間閒聊。公司裡有沒有什麼禁忌的話題呀？
April	I'm glad you asked. In general, salary is probably the one. It always causes trouble and interoffice rivalries, and hurts morale.	很高興妳問了，一般來說。薪水問題最好不要談起。這話題總是帶來麻煩，影響辦公室競爭，傷害員工士氣吶 ~
Meredith	I know what you mean. It's been a problem in almost every place I've worked.	我了解妳的意思，我以前待過的每一家公司都會因為這話題引起問題。

抓「龍」TIME

☹ Why are you here?
☺ What brings you here?
☹ Your face looks not good.
☺ You look not good.

Part III 人際

經典好用句

☺ **It's a new chapter in my career**　職場生涯中嶄新的一頁

在中文裡，我們常說是嶄新的一頁，但在英文裡習慣說是 a new chapter，也有說 a new page，但較 chapter 少。

The new peace policy is a new chapter in West Bank.
新的和平政策為約旦河西岸帶來嶄新的一頁。

☺ **May I have a word with you**　可以借一步說話嗎？

表示希望跟對方私下說話，不讓他人聽到。

（通常先說完這句，再拉對方到隱密角落去做進一步對話）

A: May I have a word with you? Peter.

B: Sure.

A: Why did you bring Kimmy to your parents' house yesterday? You know she is not welcomed.

A：Peter，可以借一步說話嗎？

B：可以啊。

A：你昨天幹嘛帶 Kimmy 去你父母家，你知道她不討人喜歡。

字彙精選

■ **a bunch of** *phr* 一群

After getting off the bus, a bunch of kids ran to the park.

下公車之後，一群小孩子跑向公園。

■ **formal** *adj* 正式的

A: Why you dressed so formal?

B: I'm going to have a job interview this afternoon.

A：你怎麼穿這麼正式？

B：今天下午要面試。

■ **punch in and out** 上班打卡

You need to punch in and out here. It's a company policy.

公司規定，上下班要打卡。

Facebook 的打卡為 check in。

I already took the pictures. Let's check in the facebook.

我拍好照了，趕快上 facebook 打卡吧。

■ **accountant** *n* 會計

Melinda is our senior accountant. She looks stern. Nobody dares talk to her.

Melinda 是我們的資深會計，她看來不苟言笑。沒人敢跟她說話。

■ **rivalry** *n* 對抗

It's a usual rivalry between Moslems and Jews.

回教徒跟基督徒常常彼此對抗。

Part III 人際

■**morale** *n* 士氣

Because of the supply shortage, the soldier morale is starting to fade away.

因為缺少補給，士兵的士氣慢慢減弱。

抓龍術大公開

1. ~~Why are~~ What brings you here?

你怎麼在這？

這一句在單獨的句子中，文法及用法其實沒有太嚴重的問題，但是在這一段對話中，當我們要問某人為什麼出現在此，比較客氣的說法，應為"What brings you here?"（什麼風把你吹來）或是"What makes you here?"（來這裡有什麼事嗎？）。

2. ~~Your face looks~~ You look not good.

你臉色看起來不太好。

這一句的錯誤說法在於以中文直譯，但在英文中卻沒有「臉色」這樣的說法。一般會說"You don't look good."或是"You look not well."來指看起來氣色不太好。在這一個句子當中，good 跟 well 沒有太大的差異，只有一點需要注意的是，"You don't look good."除了指健康狀況之外，有時也可當作是指穿著不太得體等的。

另外也可以用看起來臉色蒼白"You look pale."來形容。pale 的意思是指蒼白的，可以用來形容膚色及氣色。

例句

A: You look so pale, you should take some rest.

B: I missed my breakfast this morning. I was busy.

A：你臉色看起來蒼白，你需要休息一下。

B：我早上太忙，以致沒吃早餐。

Part III 人際

Unit 6 早退

Dialogue

April	Well, Meredith, I'd like to introduce you to our colleagues. Let's start from the Sales Department.	嗯，Meredith，我來介紹我們同事給妳認識，我們從業務部門開始吧。
Meredith	Sure, I can't wait to meet them.	當然，我等不及跟他們見面了。
April	Hi, Christina, this is Meredith. She is our new sales representative.	Hi，Christina，這位是 Meredith 她是我們的新業務。
Christina	Meredith? Is that you?	Meredith，是妳嗎？
Meredith	Oh~ Christina!! I can't believe it. She was my college classmate. Tell you something. We were roommates. There were no secrets between girls. We shared everything.	哇！Christina，真不敢相信。她是我大學同學，告訴妳，我們是室友。彼此分享秘密。

Christina	Meredith!! Wow ~ I haven't heard from you since 2012. I thought that you had moved to Houston.	Meredith！！哇～從 2012 年我就沒聽過妳的消息，我以為妳搬去 Houston。
Meredith	Yes, I did. But I moved back last year. Now I'm a freshman in the Grey Product. Any advice?	我是呀，可是我去年搬回來了，我現在是 Grey 公司的新人。有什麼建議嗎？
Christina	Well, I <u>have to</u> say. We don't talk about other people's private lives. It's kind of good rules of thumb. Speaking of private lives, interoffice romance is not a good idea, even though there is no written statement about it. But you should avoid it unless it won't affect your work performance. Gossip time, Webber married his secretary.	嗯，不得提一下，我們不討論別人的私生活，這是基本原則。說到私人生活，最好避免辦公司戀情。雖然沒有明文規定，你還是要注意，除非這不會影響你的工作表現。八卦一下，Webber 娶了他的秘書。
Meredith	☹️I don't tell anyone.	我不會告訴任何人。
April	Webber, may I come in?	Webber，我可以進來嗎？

Part III 人際

Webber	Yes, please. Where is Meredith?	好，請。Meredith 去哪裡了？
April	Well, she is in the Sales Department. <u>It turns out</u> that Christina was her college friend. I believe there is so much for them to catch up. So I left her there. Are you ok?	她在銷售部門。原來她跟 Christina 以前是大學同學。我想她們應該有很多要聊的吧。所以，我就把她留在那裡。你還好嗎？
Webber	Well, I'm much better, but I don't think I can concentrate on the work because I am still dizzy now. It's past five o'clock, so let's finish work.	嗯，我好一點了。但是我覺得還是有點頭暈，沒辦法專心工作。已經 5 點，我們可以下班了。
April	Sure, do you need a ride?	當然，需要我載你一程嗎？
Webber	Thank you, April. You have been very helpful. I'd like to take tomorrow off and see my doctor. But, I'm supposed to have an early meeting with Meredith for the pricing strategy tomorrow morning. So, can you put it off?	謝謝你，April。妳幫了大忙。我明天會請假去看醫生，但是明天早上我應該要跟 Meredith 開會討論定價策略。妳能把它延後嗎？

| April | That can be arranged. Don't worry. Just take a good rest. | 那可以安排，不要擔心，好好休息。 |

抓「龍」TIME

☹ I don't tell anyone.
☺ I won't tell anyone.
☹ Let's finish work.
☺ Let's get off work.

經典好用句

☺ **have to**　必須

I have to say Michael is our possible candidate for winning the election.
我必須說，Michael 是我們最可能獲勝的候選人

They have to stay home because of curfew.
因為宵禁，他們必須待在家裡。

☺ **it turns out that**　結果是

It turns out that the best exercise is jogging.
結果慢跑才是最好的運動。

It turns out that they both got drunk.
結果是他們兩個都醉了。

Part III 人際

字彙精選

■ **good rules of thumb**　經驗法則，好的原則

Here's a good rule of thumb: if you don't know what to say, just keep quiet!!

原則是，如果你不知道該說什麼，那就別說！！

■ **concentrate**　*v*　專注

The WHO must concentrate on the development of Ebola virus vaccination.

世界衛生組織必須專注於發展伊波拉疫苗。

■ **dizzy**　*adj*　頭暈的

After drinking the wine, Adam started to feel dizzy.

喝了那杯酒之後，Adam 覺得頭很暈。

■ **Need a ride?**　需要我載你一程嗎？

A: I feel dizzy after the drink.

B: Need a ride? I'm heading home.

A：喝了那杯酒，我頭很暈。

B：要我載你一程嗎？我正要回去。

抓龍術大公開

1. I ~~don't~~ won't tell anyone.

我不會告訴任何人。

這裡的錯誤是在於時態，因為這一件事尚未發生，而 Meredith 也是剛剛才知道這一件事，所以最好以未來式表示。而「保守秘密」其實更生動的

說法為"I'll keep it to myself."（我只留給我自己。）或是"I will hold my tongue."（我會管好我的舌頭。），這樣的說法是不是更有趣呢！

例句

　　A: Adam just had a big fight with his wife.
　　B: Well, you should keep it to yourself. I'm not interested
　　　　in his personal life.
　　A：Adam 剛剛跟他太太吵了一架
　　B：嗯，你應該什麼也別說，我對他私事沒有興趣。

2. Let's ~~finish~~ get off work.

我們可以下班了。

下班

☹finish work

☺get off work

"finish work"應解釋成完成工作，與句中的下班之意不符，所以應該用 get off work。但其實在這一種情況下，還有一種更貼切的說法，我們可以說"Let's call it a day."（今天就到此結束吧。）

例句

　　It's getting late; I'd like to call it a day. We have to catch
　　up the train tomorrow morning.
　　很晚了，我想要結束工作，回去休息了。明早還要搭火車呢。

Part III 人際

Unit 7 閒聊

Dialogue

April	Good morning, Meredith, wow~ nice dress. You look <u>stunning</u> today.	早，Meredith， 哇！好漂亮的裙子，妳今天看起來真棒。
Meredith	Thank you, <u>I'm flattered</u>. You know, my friends would never <u>think highly of</u> me in fashion aspect in the past. Vogue was never my favorite magazine. I prefer health guide to fashion magazine. However, after working here, I decide to change myself. And I have to say I really feel more confident now.	謝謝，我受寵若驚。你知道嗎？我以前的朋友覺得我對穿著上沒什麼天分。Vogue 不是我最喜歡的雜誌，我喜歡養身指南多更勝流行雜誌。但是自從在這裡上班之後，我決定改變我自己。我必須承認，我真的覺得有自信多了。

April	You should be. Especially when working in the Grey Product, a famous international cooperation. ☹You present our company while speaking to our client. They said you can't judge a person by his clothes. But the truth is fine feathers make fine birds.	沒錯！特別 Grey 是知名的國際企業。當跟客戶說話的時候，我們就代表了公司。雖說不能依衣著來評斷別人，但是人要衣裝總是真理。
Meredith	☹I agree with you very much. In certain occasions, we must pay attention to our clothes; the decent clothes make us more professional.	我十分同意。在特定場合，我們得留意自己的穿著，適當的衣著使我們看起來更專業。
April	Indeed, I have to go. Webber is waiting for me, talk to you later.	的確，我先走了，Webber 還在等我。我們晚點聊。
Christina	Hey, Meredith, here you are. I can see you get along pretty well with April.	嘿，Meredith，妳在這呀。看來妳跟 April 相處得很好哦。
Meredith	Yes, I do. Most of them are nice to me, but Carrie is not included.	是呀，大部分的人對我都不錯。除了 Carrie。

Christina	May I know why? She seems to be an attractive woman.	怎麼了，她看起來滿有魅力的呀。
Meredith	Well, I guess, that's the problem. She talked a lot behind someone's back and spread rumors among colleagues. You know she told me so much gossip about April. I've just been here for a month. I don't think she is a trustworthy person.	我想問題就在這。Carrie 在人背後議論紛紛，而且在同事間亂傳謠言，生事。你知道她跟我說了好多 April 的八卦嗎？我才來這裡上班一個月耶，我真的認為 Carrie 不是可靠的人。
Christina	Yep, you got the point. She considers herself as the queen in the office and tries to manipulate other people. Maybe we should remind April tactfully that she shouldn't share her personal life with Carrie anymore.	你看出問題所在了。Carrie 認為她是辦公室的女王，喜歡操控別人。我們應該善意的提醒 April 叫她不要跟 Carrie 講太多私人的事。
Meredith	I will. April has been so nice to me since I got here. I don't understand why Carrie is such hyper-critical.	我會的。我來上班之後，April 一直對我很好。我不懂 Carrie 幹嘛這麼愛批評人。

| Christina | April is well-liked by everyone. Maybe Carrie is jealous of her. | 大家都喜歡 April，Carrie 可能是忌妒吧。 |

抓「龍」TIME

☹ You present our company while speaking to our client.
☺ You represent our company while speaking to our client.
☹ I agree with you very much.
☺ I totally agree with you.

經典好用句

☺ **I'm flattered**　受寵若驚；過獎了

A: Your photograph is very professional.
B: Thank you, I'm flattered.
A：你的攝影作品很專業
B：謝謝，過獎了。

☺ **think highly of**　重視；對⋯⋯有很高的評價

Most families think highly of the home security.
大部分的家庭很重視居家安全。

字彙精選

■ **stunning** *adj* 令人驚艷的

The Dior latest summer collection is stunning.
Dior 最新夏季系列令人驚艷。

■ **rumor** *n* 謠言

Rumor has it that Harry's father is secretly in love with
Harry's classmate.
謠言說 Harry 的爸爸跟 Harry 的同學偷偷談戀愛。

■ **trustworthy** *adj* 值得信賴的

Sandra is a trustworthy person, and she would never betray
her friends.
Sandra 值得信賴，她從不背叛朋友。

■ **manipulate** *v* 操控

The commercial advisement is trying to manipulate public's
taste.
商業廣告想要操控大眾喜好。

■ **tactfully** *adv* 有技巧地，得體地。

He paused and thought about how to answer the question
tactfully.
他停下，想了一會該如何好好回答這個問題。

■ **critical** *adj* 愛批評的，嚴重的

His report is highly critical of the government policy.
他的報告中對政府政策諸多批評。

抓龍術大公開

1. You ~~present~~ represent our company while speaking to our client.

   當跟客戶說話的時候，我們就代表了公司。

   代表
   ☹present
   ☺represent

   present 當動詞使用時，有呈現、出現之意，容易與 represent 混淆。
   在這句子中為了表達是代表公司，應說 represent。

2. I totally agree with you ~~very much~~.

   我十分同意。

   句中如果一定要以 very much 來表達，那就請置於 agree 的前面，成
   為 "I very much agree with you."。但是一般常聽到的說法為：
   I totally agree with you. （我完全地同意你說的。）
   Can't agree with you more. （我再同意不過了。）

   例句
   > A: The Maroon 5 is the best rock band in the States.
   > B: I totally agree with you/ I can't agree with you more.
   > A：Maroon 5 是美國最棒的搖滾樂團。
   > B：你說的對極了。

Unit 8　抱怨同事

Dialogue

Kelly　We are trying to win ABC new orders, but the negotiation didn't succeed. The customer is not satisfied with our new price and they requested on Quality Check for every item before the shipment. ABC Company complained so much about our product quality. They said there were 5% defective products in last shipment. I don't think Kenny will agree to implement 100% inspection. It's a time-consuming work. Besides; Kenny is very bad to me. What do you think about Kenny?

我們正在爭取 ABC 公司的新訂單，但是，之前的貿易談判並不順利，客戶不滿意我們的價格。而且一直抱怨我們的品質有問題，他們說上次出貨有 5% 的貨有瑕疵。要求出貨前要百分百出貨前驗貨，我不認為 KENNY 會同意 100% 的驗貨。100% 驗貨實在太耗時了。此外，Kenny 對我很不好。你覺得 Kenny 這人怎樣？

Claire Kenny? The QC manager? Well, I don't know what you refer to. But Kenny has been working in the Quality Department for 3 years, and I would just like to say that I have heard nothing but positive about his performance! Actually, most employees like to work under his leadership.

嗯，我似乎不太清楚你是什麼意思，Kenny 在我們公司的品保部門任職 3 年了。對於 Kenny 的表現，我聽到的都是非常好的。事實上，大部分的員工喜歡在他的領導下工作。

Annie I totally agree with Claire. Kenny is a hard-working person. Maybe there is some misunderstanding between you and him. Maybe it's a great chance for you two to clear the air. I believe that things will work out. Just remember, you have to handle this matter very carefully.

我同意 Claire 的說法，或許你跟 Kenny 之間有什麼誤會了。這一次是很好的機會可以跟 Kenny 消除隔閡。我想事情會被解決的。但是記得，這事你要小心處理。

Kelly I know, but he rejected my proposals so many times without any reasons. Maybe he was too busy to explain to me. Thanks for the advice. I hope Kenny and I can be peaceful. If I can persuade him to accept the 100% inspection, then I bet that we can get ABC's new order.

我知道。但是他之前退回我的提案許多次了，而且沒有任何原因。或許他是太忙了，以致於沒空跟我解釋原因吧！！謝謝你們的建議。我希望我和 Kenny 能和平相處。如果我能說服他 100% 出貨前驗貨的話，那我拿到 ABC 公司的訂單機率就很高了。

Annie	That's right. Keep thinking positive and working hard. I have confidence in you. If you do, you may get a promotion next month. I heard there is a sales competition next month. The winner will win extra bonus, good luck!!	沒錯，保持正面的想法努力工作。我對你有信心，如果你真的拿到 ABC 的訂單，你下個月就可以晉升了。我聽說有個業務競賽，獲勝者還能贏得獎金呢，祝你好運！！

抓「龍」TIME

☹ Kenny is very bad to me.

☺ Kenny is very hard on me.

☹ I hope Kenny and I can be peaceful.

☺ I hope Kenny and I can get along with each other.

經典好用句

☺ **It's a time consuming work**　這是個耗時的工作。

consume 當動詞時是消費，consumer 則為衍生名詞，意思是消費者。當我們要表達「耗時」時，一般在大腦往往會直接翻為 spend a lots of time（花費很多時間）這個用法，這用字跟文法結構無誤，但是，若可以使用 time consuming ，更能表示使用者的英文水平。

Sculpture is a time consuming art. It requires lots of patience.

雕刻是門耗時的藝術，需要許多的耐心。

☺ **I totally agree with**… 我完全贊同……

十分同意對方說法是 I totally agree with you. 更口語的說是，在對方
敘述完之後說"Totally Agree!"

A: Travelling in Taiwan is very safe and convenient.

B: Totally agree!

A：在台灣旅遊十分安全跟便利。

B：我完全同意你的話。

亦有人說 I can't agree with you more.

按英文字面是「我不能同意你更多了」，意思就是我完全認同你。

字彙精選

■**negotiation**　*n*　談判

The negotiation was very successful with the client.

跟客戶的談判很順利。

■**complained**　*v*　complain的過去式；抱怨

Joe complains about his work all the time.

Joe 老是抱怨他的工作。

■**defective**　*adj*　瑕疵的

All defective items were returned to the supplier.

所有的瑕疵貨都退回給供應商了。

■**inspection**　*n*　檢驗

The new client has a high standard on quality inspection.

新客戶對品質檢驗的要求很高。

■**performance** *n* 表現

His performance in the army makes his parents so proud.
他在軍中的表現，使他的父母引以為傲。

■**employee** *n* 員工

employ v 雇用

employer n 雇主

employ 是很有趣的一個字，衍生名詞有兩種，卻是完全不一樣的意思。

The employer decided to employ a new employee.
雇主決定雇用新的員工。

抓龍術大公開

1. Kenny is very ~~bad to~~ hard on me.
Kenny對我很不好。

不好（人際上）
☹bad
☺hard

這樣的說法，比較像是幼兒在形容同儕的人際關係正確用法。在職場中人際關係中，我們常常覺得有些同事對我們很嚴或是相處不好。其實你可以這樣說"He is very hard on me."，hard 在這裡是指嚴格的。或是"I really don't know what he's thinking."。在英文裡，通常不會直接用好，壞等評論性的字眼去描述人際關係。用上述兩句就可代表其實對方不是你的好麻吉，或稱不上是朋友。

2.I hope Kenny and I can ~~be peaceful~~ get along with each other.

我希望Kenny跟我可以和平相處。

和睦相處
☹be peaceful
☺get along with each other

這也可以算是中式說法，**peaceful** 是形容詞，意思是「和平的」，通常是用在形容國際關係或是個人感受。

例句

The relationship between Taiwan and Japan is very peaceful.
台灣跟日本的關係十分的和平。

My mind is so peaceful when walking into the temple.
走進寺廟時，我感覺很平和。

在表達人與人相處的來時，比較適合的說法是 **get along with**（相處的來）

例句

I get along well with him because we all graduated from the same college.
我跟他處的來，因為我們都是同一間學校畢業的。

For some reasons, I don't get along well with him.
基於某種理由，我跟他處不來。

Unit 9　面試

Dialogue

During the interview
在面試中

David	Good afternoon, I'm very happy to be here in front of you and present myself. My name is David Chang, and I am a candidate for the position of Overseas Sales Representative.	您好，我很高興有這機會在此介紹我自己。我是 David Chang，我目前應徵的是貴公司海外業務代表一職。
Joseph	Thanks for coming. Tell us about your background, David	謝謝您的到來。David，跟我們說說你自己。
David	I graduated from NYU in 2010, and my major is International Business. For 5 years from now, I had been able to put what I've learned to good use in the ABC Product, Japan.	我在 2010 時，於 NYU 畢業，主修國際商業。從我畢業後至今約五年，我一直在日本 ABC 公司任職，在 ABC 公司將學以致用。
Joseph	ABC Product? That's a very well-known company.	ABC 公司？這是一家很知名的公司。

David　Yes, it's. I'm aware that you are expanding business into Asia market, especially in Japan. So, you will need an aggressive sales representative. At the ABC Product, during my 5 years there, we had expanded our U.S. market share by 17%. Here is the related report to show that I'm capable of expanding business.

是的，沒錯。我得知貴公司正有計畫拓展亞洲市場，尤其是日本市場。貴公司需要一個積極的業務代表。在我任職 ABC 公司的 5 年中，我們的業務成長了 17%。這裡有相關報告，可以證明我拓展市場的能力。

Joseph　Very impressive, Thank you, David. We will inform you as soon as possible.

很好，謝謝您的介紹。我們會很快的通知您結果。

After the interview
面試後

Joseph　I know there are different opinions regarding to this subject, but we need to make a conclusion on who is the best candidate to take on the position of our Overseas Sales Representative.

我知道大家對於我們討論的主題各有意見，但是今天必須我們要決定誰能勝任我們海外業務代表一職。

Part III 人際

Sophia	I had met with all the candidates. So far, I would say that David has the most impressive credentials. He is ready for the position.	面試者我都一一見過了。目前看來，David 的資歷最讓我印象深刻。我想他來做我們的海外業務應該沒有問題。
Kenny	I'm afraid that I don't agree. I've talked to David and found it difficult to communicate with him. He seems to be very stubborn. We are a team, how can I work with a stubborn person?	我不這麼想，我跟 David 聊過。我發現和他溝通有點困難，他好像有點固執。我們是一個團隊，我怎麼跟一個堅持己見的人合作？
Joseph	Kenny, don't you think that David's credentials are very qualified? He has been working for many years; I believe that PR is not a question for him. Maybe we should give him a chance to see if he can be a team player.	Kenny，你不認為 David 的資歷跟符合我們的要求嗎？他曾在職場上多年，人際關係應該不會有太大問題。或許我們可以給他個機會，看他是否能團隊合作。

抓「龍」TIME

☹ I'm happy to be here.

☺ It's a pleasure for me to be here.

☹ PR is not a question for him.

☺ PR is not a problem for him.

經典好用句

☺ **I'm aware that**… 我有注意到

I'm aware that the Japan stock has dropped 7 % since last month.

我注意到從上個月起，日本股市跌了 **7%**。

☺ **make a conclusion** 下結論

Don't make a conclusion before we have collected all the information.

在我們收集到所有資訊前，不要妄下定論。

字彙精選

■ **candidate** *n* 候選人

Francis is the new candidate for the 10th president election.

Francis 是第 10 屆的總統候選人。

■ **well-known** *adj* 有名的，眾所皆知的

The Apple cell phone is well-known in the mobile market.

Apple 的手機在手機市場中是眾所皆知的。

■ **expand** *v* 延伸

The Weather report warning:

The super storm expands from North America to Mexico, people must prepare for it.

氣象預報警告：超級風暴從北美洲延伸至墨西哥，人們必須做好準備。

■ **aggressive** *adj* 充滿野心的，具侵略性的

In the safety of road, avoiding the eye contact with aggressive drivers is necessary.

在用路安全守則上，必須避免與兇狠的駕駛的眼神接觸。

■ **credentials** *n* 資歷，多為複數

After reading Peters' resume, I have to say, his career credentials is very impressive.

看完 Peter 的履歷之後，我不得不說，他的資歷令人印象深刻。

抓龍術大公開

1. ~~I'm very happy~~ It's my pleasure to be here.
我很高興有這機會在此。

"I'm very happy to meet you."（我很高興能在這裡。），比較適用於在日常生活中。一般在正式的商業英文中，表示很高興見到對方，應該為"It's my pleasure to meet you."（很榮幸遇見您。）或是"I'm grateful to have this opportunity to be here."（我非常感激能有機會來到這裡。）

更正式的說法可為"It's my honor to meet you."意思為很榮幸遇見您，但是帶有更尊重之意。用到 My honor 通常對方多為身分重要人士或是自己已仰慕對方已久，想表達敬意。

2. PR is not a ~~question~~ problem for him.

人際關係對他而言應該不會有太大問題。

問題
☹ question
☺ problem

句中的 PR=Person Relationship，指的是人際關係。question 及 problem 都可以被視為是一個需要被解決及討論的問題。question 比較是只要一個答案就可以解決的問題，但在程度上相對來說 problem 就比較像是「難題」，比較「難以處理的事」，所以在這裡要用 problem。然而 problem 通常具有比較負面的意思，例如 "What's your problem?" 是「你有什麼毛病？」帶有找碴的意思，所以也逐漸有人在某種程度上會以 issue 來代替 problem。例如這一句就可以說是 "PR is not an issue for him."（人際關係對他不是問題。）除此之外，在商業用途中，可用 issue 表示待解決的事項。

例句

We have a new issue on the quality.
品質上有些待解決的事項 = 品質有問題。

Part III 人際

Unit 10 任職

Dialogue

David

Hi, I'm David, the new Overseas Sales Representative. I won't take up much of your time. I just want to introduce myself. I came from the ABC Product in Japan, a company you might hear before. I was responsible for the luggage exporting to the Sates. I'm very looking forward to cooperating with you.

嗨，我是 David。新的海外業務代表。我不會耽擱妳太多時間，自我介紹一下。我之前在日本 ABC 公司，或許妳有聽過這家公司。在 ABC 公司時，我負責出口行李箱到美國市場。很期待能與妳合作。

Cindy	Nice to meet you. David. I'm Cindy, I handle the Japan market. I heard about the ABC Product before. It's quite famous in this industry. I just wonder, why did you want to leave that company? I'm all ears.	歡迎你加入我們公司，我是 Cindy。我負責日本市場，我聽過 ABC 公司，在業界很有名氣。告訴我，你怎麼會想離開 ABC 公司，我願意洗耳恭聽。
David	Well, you know. It's a Japanese company. There are hundreds of regulations in the company policy. I mean everything is in the details. To me, it's never enough to check my work twice. It really took me so much time on the daily reports that I hardly left my office before 11 PM. That's really a challenge for me.	嗯，你知道的，日本公司有好多規定。我的意思是，所有的東西都要的鉅細靡遺。我每天檢查我的工作內容兩次都還不夠。但是每天花很多時間在日常報告上，以至於我晚上大概都 11 點後才能下班。這對我來說實在太辛苦了。
Cindy	Wow~ it's hard to imagine. But I heard that the wage is relatively high, isn't it?	哇～ 很難想像這樣的生活。但是聽說薪水相對很高，不是嗎？

David	Not really. Honestly speaking, we got fair salary only. But people respect you, and that's a big attraction. My health condition is the biggest issue. After 5 years in the ABC Product, my health was getting worse because I didn't have enough rest even on the weekend. I was under a lot of pressure at that period time. It's was very stressful. Then my doctor suggested that I should keep my regular work and rest time balanced.	不盡然。坦白説，我們的薪水只能算合理。但是若你在 ABC 公司上班，人們總是很敬佩你，這真的是一個很大的誘因。我想最大的原因是我的健康。在 ABC 五年之後，我的健康每況愈下，因為即使週末，我還是不能好好休息。那段時間實在壓力很大，我有點精神不好。醫生建議我應該要保持生活跟休息均衡。
Cindy	I can't agree with you anymore. Health is the foundation of our life. Tell you what, Joseph values the employee's health a lot, and our employee welfare is very good. We even have a gym on the 5th floor, and it's free. You can exercise there at any time.	你説的很對，健康是一切的基礎。告訴你，Joseph 很重視員工的健康，我們的員工福利很好的。在五樓，我們甚至有個健身中心，那是免費的。你隨時可以去那裡運動。

| David | That hears great!! I can't wait to use it. | 聽起來很棒，我等不及要使用健身中心了。 |

抓「龍」TIME

☹ I handle the Japan market.
☺ I am responsible for the Japan market.
☹ That hears great!
☺ That sounds great!

經典好用句

☺ **I'm all ears.** 洗耳恭聽

中文直譯為「我都是耳朵」，其實為洗耳恭聽。

What happened between Melody and you? I'm all ears!!
你跟 Melody 之間發生了什麼事，我洗耳恭聽。

注意：此為口語用法，若是上課，演講等重要陳述時，表達認真聽講，須使用 Listen carefully!!（認真聽講。）

☺ **that's really a challenge for me.** 對我來說是個大挑戰。

Surfing is really a challenge for me; I don't know how to keep my balance on the surfing board.
衝浪對我來說是個很大的挑戰，因為我不知道怎麼在衝浪板上保持平衡。

Part III 人際

字彙精選

■ **take up** *phr* 占用

David took up his working time on stock investment, so he got fired.

David 在上班時間炒股票,所以被解職了。

■ **honestly speaking** *phr* 老實說

Honestly speaking, I don't feel well today. I may leave the office earlier.

老實說,我今天不太舒服,我可能早退。

■ **attraction.** *n* 吸引

The scary novels always hold a special attraction for me.

恐怖小説總是很吸引我。

■ **getting worse** 越來越糟

The air pollution is getting worse in China; however, the China government doesn't take any action on this public subject.

空氣汙染在中國日趨嚴重,然而,針對此公眾議題,中國政府並未採取任何行動。

■ **stressful** *adj* 壓力沉重

Katherine feels so stressful about the new house because the mortgage loan is about USD200,000.

新房子讓 Katherine 壓力沉重,因為房屋貸款約 20 萬美金。

■ **foundation** *n* 基礎

Jack laid the foundation of his success by studying and working hard.

透過學習與努力工作,Jack 為自己的成功打下基礎。

抓龍術大公開

1. I ~~handle~~ am responsible for the Japan market.
我負責日本市場。

負責
☹handle
☺responsible for

be responsible for　為⋯⋯負責
例句

> All pilots must be responsible for passengers' safety.
> 機長須為乘客的安全負責。

2. That ~~hears~~ sounds great!
聽起來很棒！

聽起來
☹hear
☺sound

通常，我們在表達自己聽到什麼東西時，使用 hear，例如"I hear some noise from upstairs."（我聽到樓上傳來聲響。）這時用 hear 無誤。但是要表達「某某聽起來」時，則要採用 sound。

例句

> The noise from upstairs sounds creepy.
> 樓上傳來的聲響聽起來很詭異。

Unit 11 升遷

Dialogue

Joseph	Hey, Claire, have you read the latest appointment announcement?	嘿，Claire，妳看了新的人事公告了嗎？
Claire	No, I have been very busy since the morning. <u>What's up?</u>	還沒有，我早上到現在一直很忙。怎麼了？
Joseph	Well, if I were you, I would read it ASAP.	如果我是妳，我會趕快去看哦。
Claire	Wow ~ I can't believe it. I thought it would be Cindy. After all, it's amazing that she got the Toyo case. Thank you for standing behind me, Joseph. <u>That means a lot to me.</u>	哇～我真不敢相信。我以為會是 Cindy，畢竟她拿下 Toyo 案子很了不起的。謝謝你一直支持我，Joseph，這對我意義重大。

Joseph	I just did the right thing. You devote yourself on this job. Listen, there will be a small party to celebrate your promotion this afternoon, at 3 o'clock in the conference room. Get yourself ready.	我只是說出對的事情。妳一直對工作都很投入。下午 3 點在會議室有個小派對慶祝妳的升遷。準備一下。
Claire	Sure thing!!	當然沒問題。

In the conference room
在會議室

Claire	Thank you, Joseph. It's a great honor to be under your leadership and got promoted to overseas sales manager. Frankly speaking, I will take this as the recognition of our team performance; all of my co-workers are so wonderful. I can't get this promotion without your support…	謝謝，Joseph，我很榮幸跟隨您之後，成為了海外業務經理。老實說，這項升遷，我把它視為對我們團隊表現的一種肯定。我們所有的同仁都十分優秀，沒有他們的支持，我不會有這機會的……
David	Congratulations, I wish I could be as lucky as you are. Haha.	恭喜妳呀，要是我像妳一樣幸運就好了。哈哈哈！

Part III 人際

Joseph	Just don't pay attention to him, keep talking, Claire. David is not well today.	別管他,繼續説。Claire,David 今天有點怪。
Claire	Thank you, Joseph. Well, on that same note, I'd like to thank all my colleagues in the Sales Department for their enthusiasm and hard-working. Due to their continuous efforts, we've really gotten some overseas projects off the ground for action. Looking to the future, I'd still like to extend our business to more and more countries. One more thing, I'd like to bring it out especially to Cindy. She is our new partner, who got the Toyo's case last month. As you all know, it's the biggest fabric importer in Japan. That's a huge success for our team. I hope we can be as aggressive as she is.	謝謝您,Joseph,接我上面的話。我要感謝業務部同仁在工作的熱忱及辛勤。因為其不間斷的努力。我們的海外市場計畫得以漸有成效。展望未來,我希望我們能攻下更多海外市場。在此,也要特別提出,Cindy,她是我們的新夥伴,她上個月拿下 Toyo 的案子。大家都知道,Toyo 是日本最大的織布進口商。這對我們團隊來説是個巨大的成功。我希望大家都能夠和 Cindy 一樣積極。
Joseph	That's an inspiring speech, Claire. I can see the promising future of our company. Go for it!!	妳的演説十分鼓舞大家,Claire,我能預見公司的未來充滿潛力。大家一起努力。

抓「龍」TIME

☹ Don't pay attention to him.
☺ Ignore him.
☹ David is not well today.
☺ David is not himself today.

經典好用句

☺ **what's up** 怎麼了？有什麼事嗎？

多為在輕鬆愉快的氣氛下，詢問對方有什麼事的問句？表示有什麼鮮事嗎？

A: Hey, Kevin, I haven't seen you since yesterday.
B: What's up?
A: We have a party tonight, and you should go with me.
A：Kevin 我從昨天就沒看到你了
B：什麼事情？
A：我們今晚有個派對，你應該跟我一起去。

若是感覺有些不對勁時的問句，則應該為"What's the matter?"

A: Why you look so upset? What's the matter?
B: I can't find my luggage!!
A：你怎麼看起來這麼不開心，發生什麼事了？
B：我找不到我們行李！

☺ **that means a lot to me** 對我意義重大

The family support means a lot for Jackson. They are very close to each other.
家庭的支持對 Jackson 而言十分重要，他們很親近。

字彙精選

■ **recognition** *n* 認可

Sandra's outstanding performance has received supervisor's recognition.

Sandra 傑出的工作表現，得到了上司的認可。

■ **same note** 一樣的氣氛，印象

On the same note, I like to stress on the importance of the replacement resource.

同之前說的，我想要強調再生能源的重要性。

■ **enthusiasm** *n* 熱情，熱衷

Owen has enthusiasm for Taekwondo, so he has taken Taekwondo class for two years.

Owen 對跆拳道十分熱衷，他學了兩年的跆拳道課程。

■ **continuous** *adj* 不間斷的，持續的

We are seeking a continuous and incremental improvement rather than a great breakthrough.

我們尋求的是不間斷及漸進式的改善而不是要重大的突破。

■ **get off the ground** 有所進展

After 11 years, the Mars mission is finally getting off the ground.

經過 11 年，火星任務終於有所進展。

■ **inspiring** *adj* 激勵人心

Mr. Lee's speech was so inspiring that people started to donate money.

李先生的演講太激勵人心了，人人紛紛開始捐錢。

抓龍術大公開

1. ~~Don't pay attention to him~~ Ignore him.
   不要管他。

   pay attention to（留意）在此不適用。應改用 ignore（忽略）。正確
   用法可說"Ignore him."或是"Leave him alone."。

   例句

   > A: Jimmy is grumpy today, what happened?
   > B: I don't know, just ignore him.
   > A：Jimmy 今天脾氣很怪，發生什麼事了？
   > B：我不知道，別理他。

2. David is not ~~well~~ himself today.
   David 今天怪怪的。

   在情境對話中，David 在 Claire 發言時大吵大鬧，表現不當。為緩和
   氣氛，Joseph 說了"David is not well today."但這一句應被解釋
   成「David 今天生病了」，並不太符合對話內容。應改成"He is not
   himself today."或是"He is not acting like himself."，意思為「他
   今天不是他自己。」或是「他平常不會這樣的。」此句較有緩和之意，表
   示 David 平時不是這樣愛吵鬧的，他只是有點失常。

   例句

   > A: Adam got drunk on my birthday party, and he said
   >   something stupid.
   > B: Don't blame him. He was not himself.
   > A：Adam 在我生日派對上喝醉了，說了些蠢話。
   > B：不要怪他，他那天有點失常。

Unit 12 下午茶

Claire	Cindy, I want to have some coffee downstairs, come with me?	Cindy，我想去樓下喝點咖啡，一起去嗎？
Cindy	Sure, it's a sleepy afternoon. I could use some coffee.	好呀，令人昏昏欲睡的下午，我需要一點咖啡。
Barista	May I help you?	要點餐嗎？
Cindy	Yes, I'd like a tall mocha for here.	是的，我想要一杯中杯摩卡，這裡用。
Barista	Do you like whipped cream on your mocha.	摩卡上要加鮮奶油嗎？
Cindy	Yes, please.	好的，謝謝。
Barista	Are you ready to order? What can I get for you?	要點餐了嗎？請問要什麼？

Claire	Do you have any decaf coffee?	你們有低咖啡因咖啡嗎？
Barista	Yes, we do. We can make all our coffee drinks caffeine-free.	有的，所有的咖啡都可做低咖啡因。
Claire	Ok, I'd like a grande, iced decaf coffee for here, and ham cheese croissant. Can you please cut it into half.	好的，我要一杯大杯冰的，低咖啡因咖啡，這裡用。還有火腿起司可頌，可以幫我對切嗎？
Barista	Sure can.	沒問題。
David	Do you mind if I join you?	不介意的話，我可以跟妳們一起坐嗎？
Claire	In fact, yes, we do. It's girls' talk.	事實上，我們很介意。這是女生在閒聊。
Cindy	Haha, I can't believe that. Claire. You just rejected David in public. It's kind of embarrassing; I hope it won't provoke his anger.	哈哈！真不敢相信，Claire 妳在大庭廣眾下拒絕 David。那真糗，希望他不會惱羞成怒。
Claire	Don't worry, he will be fine.	別擔心，他沒事的。

Part III 人際

Cindy	May I know why you and David can't get along well? It seems that there must be some misunderstanding between you and David.	為什麼妳跟 David 處不好呢？能告訴我原因嗎？妳們之間好像有什麼誤會。
Claire	Well, That's a long story. In his opinion, I don't deserve this promotion. He insisted that you were the best candidate for the sales manager. However, Joseph and Sophia voted for me. He can't change the result, but he wants to prove that he's right. So, he keeps talking to me about this. <u>That's annoying.</u>	說來話長。在他看來，我不夠格當業務經理。他覺得妳才是最佳人選。可是，Joseph 跟 Sophia 投票給我。David 改變不了結果，但是他一直要證明他是對的。不斷的來跟我說這件事，真是很煩。
Cindy	Wow~ I didn't know that. Don't worry; your secret is safe with me. I will keep it to myself.	哇，我不知道此事。別擔心，我會保守妳的秘密，不跟別人說的。
Claire	On the contrary, you don't have to. He already made his point very clear at the party. Now, everyone in the office knows it.	正好相反，妳不用這麼做。他在派對上已經到處講了，所有的人都知道了。

Cindy	That's horrible, how can you focus on work when there is some backbiting around.	太可怕了，這樣妳怎麼工作？一直有人到處說妳壞話。
Claire	Indeed, but I try to ignore him. And hopefully, he can face the music soon.	的確如此，我先不理他，希望他能早日認清事實。

抓「龍」TIME

☹ It's a sleepy afternoon.
☺ It's a somnolent.

經典好用句

☺ **I could use some**… 我需要一點……（意思是本來沒有，正需要）

A: Hey, the box is heavy; let me help you with that.
B: Thank, I could use some help.
A：嘿，那箱子很重，讓我幫你拿吧。
B：謝謝，我正需要幫忙。

☺ **that's annoying** 那很煩人

The phone keeps ringing. That's annoying. I can't concentrate on the study.
電話一直響，實在很煩人，我無法專心讀書。

Part III 人際

字彙精選

■ **barista** *n* 咖啡師

To our surprise, Seven gave up his financial job and became a barista.

讓我們大吃一驚的是 Seven 放棄他財務方面的工作，成為咖啡師傅。

■ **whipped cream** *n* 打泡的鮮奶油

No whipped cream on my coffee please. I'm on diet.

我咖啡上不要放鮮奶油，我在節食。謝謝。

■ **croissant** *n* 可頌

I had a cup of coffee and some croissant for breakfast.

早上我吃了點可頌跟喝杯咖啡當早餐。

■ **provoke** *v* 激怒，引發

Don't provoke him to anger. He would turn.

不要激怒他，他會變身。

■ **contrary** *n/adj/adv* 相反的

Contrary to his wish, Melinda didn't show up in that party.

與他的期待相反，Melinda 並沒有在派對上出現。

■ **backbiting** *n* 毀謗

Kevin may face the charge of backbiting.

Kevin 可能因為毀謗而被起訴。

抓龍術大公開

1. It's a ~~sleepy~~ somnolent afternoon.
令人昏昏欲睡的下午。

昏昏欲睡
☹sleepy
☺somnolent

sleepy 必須以人當主詞，例如 I'm sleepy.（我想睡了。）若要形容其他，建議使用 somnolent。

例句

It's a somnolent Monday afternoon. I need some coffee.
星期一的下午，令人昏昏欲睡，我需要一些咖啡。

Part IV

其他

Miscellaneous

Unit 1 計程車

Driver	Morning, sir, where do you want to go?	早安，請問您要去哪裡？
Johnson	To the Opera Hotel, please.	請帶我去 Opera 飯店。
Driver	Sir, please put your seat belt on.	好的，先生。請繫上安全帶。
Johnson	How long will it take to the hotel?	去 Opera 飯店大概多久時間？
Driver	It will be about 30 minutes if we don't get stuck in the traffic jam. There is construction 2 blocks away, and now it's rush hour. Believe me, dude, you don't want to get stuck in there.	如果我們沒有被困在車陣中，應該 30 分鐘就到了。前面兩個路口，有工程在進行。現在是交通尖峰時間，相信我老兄，你不會想塞在車陣中的。
Johnson	I don't want that, too.	我也不想呀。

Driver	Don't worry, I'll make a detour; it will save us much time.	別擔心，我會繞過工程，這樣我們可以省很多時間。
Johnson	Yes, I'm in a hurry, please drive a bit faster.	好的，我趕時間，請開快一點。
Driver	Don't be so stiff, we can arrive in 30 minutes. You look so melancholy. Important meeting, huh?	放輕鬆，我們30分鐘可以抵達。你看來心事重重，是重要的會議嗎？
Johnson	Not really. My family and I are on vacation, and we plan to Macau this morning. However, when we arrived at the wharf and prepared for the Customs Inspection, we found out that our passports were left in the hotel. Can you believe that? We can't cancel the Macau hotel reservation. The hotel fare is repaid on the Internet. Therefore, the only way is that I have to go back to the hotel and get our passports, my wife and kids are waiting for me in the wharf.	不算是。我跟家人在度假，本來今天早上要去Macau。但是我們到碼頭時準備過海關時才發現護照留在飯店裡。你能相信嗎？預定的飯店不能取消，因為我們已經在網路上付清房費了。唯一的方法是，我回飯店拿護照，我太太跟小孩在碼頭等我。

Driver	☹️ We arrive. It took us only 20 minutes.	我們到了，只花了 20 分。
Johnson	Thank you so much. You are such a life saver. Can you wait for me in front of the Lobby? I'll be back very soon; I just grab the passports and then head to the wharf.	太感謝你了，你幫我個大忙。可以麻煩你在大廳前等我們，我很快拿了護照就下來，然後再趕回碼頭。
Driver	Sure! I'll be here.	好的，當然。
Johnson	Dude, I got the passports. Let's go.	老兄，我拿到護照了，我們走吧。
Driver	Ok. But I just heard it on the radio that there is a serious traffic accident on the highway. To clear the scene, the police already blocked the highway. I think we can take I-94 instead of I-86, and you can still arrive the wharf in time.	好，但是我剛剛在收音機聽到，高速公路上有嚴重事故。警方已經封鎖高速公路來清理現場。我們可以走 94 號道，不要走 86 號道。這樣你還是可以及時回到碼頭。
Johnson	You are the boss as long as you can get me there in time.	只要我能趕上，你說的算！！

抓「龍」TIME

☹ I don't want that, too.
☺ I don't want that, either.
☹ We arrive.
☺ Here we are.

經典好用句

☺ **don't be so stiff** 放鬆點

Don't be so stiff
= Loose up
= Take it easy
Don't be so stiff , we are on vacation. You should put all your work behind.
放鬆點，我們正在度假，你應該將工作拋到腦後。

☺ **as long as**… 只要

You can stay in my place as long as you like.
你愛在我家待多久，就待多久。

Part IV 其他

字彙精選

■ **stuck in** 困住

Last New Year vacation, we were stuck in the traffic for 2 hours.

上次新年假期，我們被困在車陣中兩個鐘頭。

■ **dude** *n* 老兄

Hey ! Dude, don't park in front of my house. You are blocking the exit.

嘿，老兄！ 不要把車停在我家前面，你擋住出口了。

■ **make a detour** 繞路

There is an anti-nuclear demonstration 2 blocks away, you should make a detour. 前面兩個路口有反核遊行，你應該要繞路。

■ **melancholy** *adj/n* 憂心忡忡

When thinking of his family in Syria, Mohamed's mood is full of melancholy. 當想到敘利亞的家人時，Mohamed 就顯的憂心忡忡。

■ **wharf** *n* 碼頭

Fisherman's Wharf is a hot spot in San Francisco; Jack went to there last year.

舊金山的漁人碼頭是著名景點，Jack 去年特地去了一去。

■ **head to** *phr* 前往

Where is this train heading to?

這火車開往哪裡？

抓龍術大公開

1. I don't want that, ~~too~~ either.
我也不想這樣。

也（用於否定句中）
☹too
☺either

"too"是表示肯定「也」。放在肯定句中，例如
I'm going to China next month, too. （我下個月也去大陸。）
若要表示否定句的「也」，則用 either，這一個句子中有 don't，為否定句，所以應該用 either 而非 too。

2. ~~We arrive~~. Here we are.
我們到了。

要用以表達我們抵達了，其通順及更道地的說法應為 "Here we are."
（我們到這裡了。）
另外我們還常常會說 "Here you are."，其用途十分的廣泛，但依情境不同，則有不同解釋。例如當司機在你到目的地時說的 "Here you are."，意思是：你到目的地了。而當服務生端菜上桌時說的 "Here you are." 意思是：你的菜到了。而在給別人東西時，也可以說 "Here you are."，有交到你手上的意思。

Unit 2　展場攤位

Liang	Excuse me, I'm Peter Liang from Bella Tire, Taiwan. Do you know where I can find my booth?	打擾了，我是台灣 Bella 輪胎的 Peter Liang。請問我們的攤位在哪裡？
Receptionist	☹Welcome you to our exhibition. Mr. Liang, let me see, your booth is E24. It's down that way. And here is a map of the exhibition hall; it will be helpful for you.	梁先生，歡迎您來我們的展覽會。我看看，你的攤位是 E24，從這邊往下走。這是展覽大廳地圖，對您很有幫助的。
Liang	Our samples were sent from Taiwan a month ago, did they arrive here?	我們一個月前從台灣寄出的樣品送到了嗎？

Receptionist	Wait a moment, please. Let me check our list. Well, are those big tires? They are quite impressive; those samples arrived here yesterday evening. They are in the storage area now; our staff will send them to your booth before 12 PM You don't have to worry about it.	等一下，我查看清單。是那些大輪胎嗎？真是讓人印象深刻。這些樣品昨天下午送來了，目前在儲藏室。我們的員工會在明天中午 12 點前送到您的攤位上，您別擔心。
Liang	Please make sure the delivery will be on time. I need to set up everything today. The exhibition starts tomorrow morning. By the way, is there any equipment office? I'm afraid there is a problem with the plug.	請確認要準時送達，展覽明天一早就開始了，我今天要把攤位布置好。這裡有器材室嗎？ 我的插頭有點問題。
Receptionist	All of our technicians are busy at the moment; let me make a phone call. Ok, one of our technicians will help with your problem in 10 minutes. E24? Right?	目前我們的技師都在忙，我打電話問問看。好的，有位技師 10 分鐘內可以來幫忙，E24 攤位是嗎？

Liang	I'm very concerned about the plug problem. Tomorrow is the opening day!!	我很擔心插頭的問題，展覽明天就要開始了。
Technician	Well, the plug doesn't fit the socket. It's the European socket, can't you see it? All you need is a plug adapter.	嗯，你的插頭跟插座不合。這是歐洲插座，你看不出來嗎？有個轉接器就沒問題了。
Liang	Oh~ no. I'm in serious trouble. I didn't notice the difference of 2 sockets. It's my first time for the exhibition. Where can I get the plug adapter now?	什麼～太糟了，這下麻煩了。我沒有注意到 2 種插座的不同，這是我第一次來參展。現在我到哪去找轉接器？
Technician	Sir, relax. I'm here to help, I can fix it up. I'll be back in a few minutes.	先生，先別緊張。我來幫忙的，我應該可解決這問題，我一會兒回來。
Technician	Here you go, the plug adapter. It's an international show; we have people from all over the world. It's necessary to have plug adapters in our toolbox. Now your computer works fine.	好了，轉接頭在這。這是一個國際性展覽，我們的客戶來自全世界，在我們的工具箱總是備有轉接頭的。現在，你的電腦可以正常運作了。

| Liang | Thank you so much. I'd better start to set up the booth ASAP. | 真的很感謝你，我最好開始布置我的攤位了。 |
| Technician | You bet. | 的確如此。 |

抓「龍」TIME

☹ Welcome you to our exhibition.

☺ Welcome to our exhibition.

☹ I didn't notice the difference of 2 sockets.

☺ I didn't notice the difference between 2 sockets.

經典好用句

☺ **I'm afraid there is a problem with**　恐怕……有問題

當提出問題或是抱怨時，以 I'm afraid… 為開始（我想……），是客氣的說法，有使語氣緩和的作用。

I'm afraid there is a problem with your product. It's broken.

我想你們的產品有點問題，它已破損。

☺ **you bet**　當然是

等同表示對方的說法，以肯定的語氣，口語的回話。有"當然，那還用你說"的意思。

A: I think we should pull over and get some food.

B: You bet.

A：我想我們應該路邊停車吃點東西。

B：當然好。

字彙精選

■ **booth** *n* 攤位，電話亭

Our booth in the exhibition is set up already.

我們在展覽的攤位已經布置好了。

■ **equipment** *n* 設備

The thief destroyed police electronic surveillance equipment.

那個小偷破壞了警方的電子監控設備。

■ **technician** *n* 技工

The technician is busy repairing the DVD player.

技工正忙著修理 DVD 播放器。

■ **socket** *n* 插座

For your safety, never overload an electrical socket.

為了你的安全，不要使插座電源超載。

■ **adapter** *n* 轉接器

You need an adapter for this socket.

你需要在這插座上使用個轉接頭。

■ **fix up** 修理，安排

Kenny bought a used car last month; he planned to fix it up.

Kenny 上個月買了部二手車，他打算將那台車整理整理。

抓龍術大公開

1. Welcome ~~you~~ to our exhibition.

歡迎您來我們的展覽會。

歡迎您來

☹Welcome you to⋯

☺Welcome to⋯

中文裡説的歡迎你，很直覺會脱口成 Welcome you to⋯，其中的 you 是多餘的。正確用法只要説 Welcome to⋯即可。

例句

A: Welcome to our new house. You are our first guest!!

B: Wow~ I am so flattered, you are too kind.

A：歡迎來我家，你是我們的第一組客人。

B：哇～我真是受寵若驚，你太好了。

2. I didn't notice the difference ~~of~~ between 2 sockets.

我沒注意到2個插座的不同。

⋯⋯物品間的不同

☹difference of

☺difference between

要説某某物品的不同時，應該是用 difference between⋯

例句

A: Excuse me, can you tell me the difference between those 2 items? They look so similar.

B: This one is shampoo, and the other is conditioner.

A：請問一下，這兩項東西有什麼不同嗎？他們看起來都好類似。

B：這罐是洗髮精，另外一罐是護髮乳。

Unit 3　行李遺失

 Dialogue

In the Immigration stop.
在出入境管理站。

Officer	Passport, please. What is the purpose of your visit?	請出示護照，來訪目的為何？
Keith	I'm here for the Auto Expo in downtown.	來看汽車展覽的。
Officer	Do you have an invitation? How long will you stay?	有邀請函嗎？預計停留幾天？
Keith	Here is the invitation. I will stay here for 7 days.	邀請函在這，預計停留7天。
Officer	May I see your return ticket?	我可以看你的回程票嗎？
Keith	Here, it's the e-ticket. I've printed it out.	在這裡，是電子機票，我把它印出來了。
Officer	Do you have anything to declare?	有什麼要申報的嗎？

Keith	Yes, I'm a businessman. I carry some cash, and it's about USD$ 20,000. I have filled out the declaration card.	有的，我是商人。身上帶有 20,000 美元現金。申報單我已經寫好了。
Officer	Ok, welcome to Amsterdam.	好的，歡迎來阿姆斯特丹。
Keith	Thank you	謝謝。

In the baggage process center.
在入境行李提取大廳。

Keith	Excuse me, where is the luggage carousel? My flight number is GT508.	請問，行李轉盤在哪裡？我航班號是 GT508。
Clerk	Flight GT508. Your luggage is on carousel 7.	航班 GT508 在 7 號轉盤。
Keith	Excuse me. I have been waiting for an hour. Everyone already got their luggage and left. Now the carousel is empty, but both of my bags was not on the carousel.	請問，我已等了一個小時了，所有的人都領到他們的行李也離開了。轉盤上空蕩蕩的，但是我還有兩件行李沒到。

Part IV 其他

Clerk	Ok, you need to go to the baggage claim office and fill out the lost luggage form. The baggage claim counter for GOTO Airline is over there, the green counter.	你去行李招領中心填表格，GOTO 航空的行李招領中心櫃檯在那邊。綠色那個櫃台。
Keith	Do you think they'll find my luggage?	你覺得他們找得到我的行李嗎？
Clerk	Don't worry. They usually find them within a day and deliver them straight to your hotel.	別擔心，通常一天之內就會找到，然後直接送到你的飯店去。
Keith	Thanks, <u>it's quite a relief to hear that.</u>	聽你這麼一說我就放心了。

At the baggage claim counter.
在行李領取櫃臺

Keith	Excuse me. I can't find my luggage; I'd like to file a missing luggage claim.	請問一下，我找不到我的行李了。我要填寫行李遺失單。
Clerk	Please present your baggage receipt? Let me see… <u>It appears that</u> your luggage has been delayed.	請出示您的行李收據，我查看看。看來你的行李延誤了。

Keith	Oh ~ No. How could that be? ☹ I'm bad lucky today.	不～怎麼會這樣。我今天運氣很不好。
Clerk	Relax. It happens. The good news is they are on another plane, and will arrive in the next hour, it's pretty soon. I suggest that you can wait here.	放心，好消息是，它們正在飛機上，再一小時就到了，還滿快的。我建議你在這等。
Keith	It looks like I don't have any choice.	看來我沒什麼選擇。

抓「龍」TIME

☹ Both of my bags was not on the carousel.
☺ Neither of my bags was not on the carousel.
☹ I'm bad lucky today.
☺ I'm unlucky today.

經典好用句

☺ **it's quite a relief to hear that**　聽到就放心多了

A: Michael is coming back safely from Nepal.

B: I was worried; it's quite a relief to hear that.

A：Michael 從尼泊爾安全歸來。

B：我還在擔心，聽到這消息就放心多了。

☺ **it appears that**　看起來似乎是……

It appears that Meredith would change her mind. She might move to D.C. with her husband.

看起來 Meredith 可能改變主意，她可能跟她先生搬去 D.C.。

字彙精選

■ **officer** *n* 警官，官員

The night duty officer heard some creepy sound.

值夜班的警官聽到了毛骨悚然的聲音。

■ **declare** *v* 申報

You have to declare that you are married at local authority.

你必須跟當地政府申報你已婚。

■ **carousel** *n* 轉盤

Many travelers don't know how to find their luggage carousel.

很多旅行者不知道去哪找行李轉盤。

■ **straight** *adj/adv* 直接的

It's very rude to look straight at people. You need to stop.

一直盯著人家看很沒有禮貌，不要這樣做。

■ **present** *v* 表現，提出

The school presents an opportunity to experience free music class.

學校提供一個免費體驗音樂課程的機會。

■ **baggage receipt** 行李收據

在行李 check in 之後，地勤人員會給一張小小的收據，夾在護照上，即為行李收據。

Here is your baggage receipt.

這是你的行李收據。

抓龍術大公開

1. ~~Both~~ Neither of my bags was not on the carousel.
我兩件行李都不在轉盤上。

兩者都不
☹both
☺neither

當要表示兩者皆不是，應使用 **neither**，而非 **both**。

例句

Neither of them is single. They both got married 3 years ago.
她們兩位都非單身，她們 **3** 年前結婚了。

2. I'm ~~bad lucky~~ unlucky today.
我今天很倒楣

倒楣
☹bad lucky
☺unlucky

"lucky"的意思是好運的、幸運的，做形容詞使用，以 **bad lucky** 來表示壞運並不正確，**lucky** 的反義字可以說 **unlucky**，有不幸運的、不順利的、或是倒楣的意思。其他常聽到有關「我今天很倒楣。」的說法還有："It's not my lucky day."或是"It's not my day."。

例句

It's not my day. I missed the bus this morning, and was
hit by a car this afternoon.

我今天很倒楣，早上錯過公車，下午還被車撞。

Unit 4 飯店訂房

Dialogue

On the phone
在電話中

Hotel Staff	Good morning. It's Jennifer of Royal King Hotel, how can I help you?	早安,我是皇家國王的 Jennifer,請問有什麼能為您服務的呢?
Keith	Hi, I'd like to book a single room from 2/25 to 2/28.	我想預定 2/25-2/28 一間單人房。
Jennifer	Sir, I'm afraid that we don't have single rooms from 2/25 to 2/28. Do you like to book a double room instead?	先生,很抱歉。2/25-2/28 單人房沒有了。您要改訂雙人房嗎?
Keith	Ok, I will take the double room. What's the rate for these 4 nights?	好吧。就訂雙人房。四晚上總共多少錢。
Jennifer	That will be total USD$ 400.	一共是美金 400 元。
Keith	That sounds reasonable. Is breakfast included?	聽起來很合理,有附早餐嗎?

Jennifer	Yes, Sir. The breakfast is included. What's your name?	有的，早餐含在房費裡。請問您大名是？
Keith	Please make the reservation under Keith C. Sardo.	請登記在 Keith C. Sardo 名下。
Jennifer	Sure, sir. And thanks for your call.	好的，沒問題。謝謝您的來電。

At the Hotel
在飯店

Keith	Hi, I have a reservation under the name Keith C. Sardo.	你好，我有訂房，登記名為 Keith C. Sardo。
Hotel Staff	Let me check⋯ Yes, Mr. Keith C. Sardo, you had booked a double room for 4 nights. Would you please fill out this form first?	讓我看看，有的 Mr. Keith C. Sardo。您訂了四晚上的雙人房。請您先填寫這張表格。
Keith	Can I extend my stay at this hotel for 2 more nights, please?	可以幫我再延 2 個晚上嗎？

Part IV 其他

Hotel Staff	Let me see⋯ Sure, 2 more nights. That will be totally 6 nights. I guess you are in town for the Import and Export Fair.	好的,讓我查查看。可以再為您延兩晚。一共是 6 個晚上。我猜您是來參加市裡的舉辦的進出口展覽會。
Keith	Yep, you are right. Can't miss the biggest exhibition in the Auto industry. By the way, there will be 3 guests visiting me this afternoon. Do you have lounge bar at the hotel?	沒錯,不能錯過世界上最大的汽車展。 對了,今天下午,會有 3 組客戶來拜訪我。飯店裡有酒吧嗎?
Hotel Staff	Yes, the lounge bar – Blue Moon – is on the 2nd floor. You can meet with your guests there. Do you need a taxi to the Fair tomorrow morning?	有的,我們的藍月酒吧在二樓。您可在那裡與客戶會面。您還需要明天一早去會展中心的計程車嗎?
Keith	Yes, please arrange the taxi. I will be ready around 8 AM. Thank you. You have been very helpful.	是的,請幫我安排,我大概 8 點左右出發。謝謝你的幫忙。
Hotel Staff	It's my pleasure! Enjoy your stay!	很榮幸為您服務,希望您住的愉快。

抓「龍」TIME

☹ We don't have single rooms.
☺ We don't have any single rooms left.
☹ What's your name?
☺ May I have your name, please?

經典好用句

☺ **I'd like to**⋯　我想要……

"I'd like to"跟"I want to"的意思一樣，都是我想要……，不過，I'd like to 聽起來較為客氣，是修飾的語態。

I'd like to book a double room on April 09.
我想要預約 4 月 9 號雙人房一間。

☺ **What's the rate?**　費用多少

通常詢問價格，我們直覺會用 How much⋯，但是"how much"多用於購物，例如：

How much is the dress?（這件洋裝多少錢？）
然而，How much 並不適合用於詢問房費。一般來説，飯店的費用，我們會使用以 rate 來做詢問。

What's the rate for the double room per night?
雙人房一晚的費用是多少？

字彙精選

■ **book** *v* 預訂

學校裡教的 book，書。在商業英文中卻常常是代表另一個意思，並十分重要。book 當動詞，為預訂之意。

I'd like to book a single room on August 18th.

我想要預訂 8 月 18 號雙人房一間。

You should book the S/O ASAP. The container will be ready next week.

貨櫃下週就可準備出貨，你應該要儘快預定船艙。

■ **reasonable** *adj* 合理的

This hotel rate is very reasonable; I will recommend it to my colleague.

這間飯店的價格很合理，我會推薦我同事這間飯店。

■ **reservation** *n* 保留、預約

Sorry, I can't find your reservation on the list. Let me check it again.

抱歉，我在名單上找不到您的訂位，請讓我再查查看。

■ **fill out** 填寫

通常填寫表格該用 fill out，而不是 write 寫。

You should fill out a form when checking in the hotel.

飯店登記住宿時，應該要填寫登記表。

■ **exhibition** *n* 展覽

The 6th Computer Exhibition will be held in the World Trade Center from June 1 to June 14. Don't miss it.

第六屆電腦展將於 6 月 1 號至 14 號在世貿中心展出。別錯過了！

■**lounge bar** *n* 酒吧

一般稍有規模飯店都設有酒吧。下榻的旅客可約各個當地供應廠商到飯店的 **Lounge Bar** 商談事項，以免去奔波之苦，亦可節省時間，且較容易在出差時，跟更多的不同廠商會面。

抓龍術大公開

1. We don't have any single rooms left.

我們沒有單人房了。

"We don't have single rooms."意思應解釋成沒有供應單人房，意指在飯店中沒有單人房的房型，但依照對話中上下文解釋，應該是指預定的時間內，所有的單人房已被預約。也可以説是"The single room is not available."。

available adj 可獲得的

例句

The Onion soup is not available; would you like to try others? We have fish soup.

我們沒有洋蔥湯了，您要試試別的嗎？ 我們還有魚湯。

2. ~~What's your name?~~ May I have your name, please?

請問您大名是？

原句其實更貼切中譯為「你叫什麼名字？」，但要記住一點，在職場中，大多不會這樣詢問客戶，因為這樣太直白了，甚至會被認為有點沒禮貌。除了問"May I have your name, please?"也可以説"Your name? Sir."。

而一般在電話中，若要詢問對方是誰，也不能説"What's your name?"，正確説法為："Who's calling, please?"（誰在電話上？）

Unit 5
在攤位中的介紹

Dialogue

Liang　Good morning sir, I'm Peter Liang, the sales representatives of Bella tires. I see you are looking at our tire. Its' our best-selling tire, the AW agriculture tire. It's very durable and with a competitive price. Here, take a catalog. This will show you why AW agriculture is the best choice for your company.

早安，先生，我是 Peter Liang，Bella 輪胎的業務代表。我看到您對我們的輪台有興趣。這是我們最暢銷的輪胎，AW 農業胎。AW 農業胎十分的耐用，且價格合理。來，這裡有目錄，您可以看看為什麼 AW 農業胎是您最好的選擇。

Keith　It looks very powerful and impressive. Could you tell me about your company? Bella tires? I'm not sure if I met you before.

這輪胎看起來很有力，且讓人印象深刻。可以說說你們公司嗎？Bella 輪胎，我不確定是否有聽過這名字。

Liang	Honestly speaking, it's the first exhibition we attend; we are a professional tire manufacturer. Our company was built in 1975 ; we focus on the technical development, no promotion for a long time. Now, we will devote to promoting our product. To achieve this goal, we create our exclusive own brand name, Bella tire.	坦白說,這是我們公司第一次參展。我們是專業的輪胎製造商,公司成立於 1975 年。 長期以來,我們一直致力於技術研發,而不是行銷。現在,我們決定投入行銷產品,為此,我們創立了獨家品牌,Bella 輪胎。
Keith	Sounds great, but have your product been exported to other countries? What did your customer say?	聽起來不錯。但是你們有其他國家的出口經驗嗎? 你們客戶評價如何?
Liang	That's a good question. I can see your worry, sir. Yes, we did export to many other countries, such as New Zealand, Australia, Canada, and South Africa. There is no doubt that my clients are very satisfied with our tire performance and our service. For the moment, our agriculture tire has taken the lead in our product. Please take a seat, let me demonstrate our products to you in detail. Your name, sir?	這是一個好問題,我能理解您的顧慮。我們有出口到許多其他國家,如紐西蘭,澳洲,加拿大跟南非。 毫無疑問的,我們的客戶對我們的輪胎十分滿意,對我們的服務也是讚譽有加。目前,農業胎在我們的產品線上銷售領先。請坐,我來為您詳細的展示我們產品,請問您大名是?

Part IV 其他

· 273 ·

Keith	I'm Keith, also from South Africa.	我是 Keith，我也是南非來的。
Liang	South Africa? What a coincidence. In fact, we have a client from South Africa, Lion Product. They imported 2 x 40 containers of AW agriculture tire last month.	南非，好巧。事實上，我們有個客戶 Lion，他也是南非公司。上個月他們才進口兩只 40 呎櫃的 AW 農業胎。
Keith	Lion Product? Yes, I have heard about them, but you know South Africa is a very big country; we basically are in a different market and area. But I can assume that you are very familiar with our import regulation.	Lion？我聽過這家公司。不過你也知道南非國土廣大，我們基本不在同一個市場區域裡。但是，我猜你們公司對南非的進口規定一定很熟吧。

抓「龍」TIME

☹ Our company was built in 1975.
☺ Our company was established in 1975.
☹ I can see your worry.
☺ I can see your concern.

經典好用句

☺ **I'm not sure if**　我不確定是否……

Excuse me, we want to go to the city library, but I'm not sure if I'm in the right direction.

抱歉，我們要去市立圖書館，但是我不確定我的方向是否正確。

☺ **there is no doubt**　毫無疑問的

There is no doubt that Copenhagen is my favorite city.

毫無疑問的，哥本哈根是我最喜歡的城市。

字彙精選

■ **agriculture**　*n*　農業

Agriculture is the foundation of a country.

農業為立國之本。

■ **devote to**　*v*　致力於

Professor Chamber has devoted most of his time to researching. dinosaurs for decades.

數十年來，Chamber 教授一直致力於研究恐龍。

■ **take the lead**　取得領先地位

The United States takes the lead in medical research.

美國在醫療研究上取得領先地位。

■ **demonstrate**　*v*　展示

The China government demonstrated its powerful military to the world.

中國政府向世界展示其強大的軍事力量。

Part IV 其他

■ **be familiar with**　熟悉……

We are not familiar with the immigration laws. Perhaps we need a consult.

我們對移民法並不熟悉，或許我們需要律師的幫忙。

■ **regulation**　*n*　法規

The result proves that the China regulation of copyright is inadequate.

結果顯示中國智慧財產權的法規不夠完善。

抓龍術大公開

1. Our company was ~~built~~ established in 1975.

我們公司成立於1975年。

成立
☹build
☺establish

"build"為建立，但通常是指建築物，如：

The house was built in 2006.（那棟房子建立於 2006 年。）

若是要說明公司成立，或是建立某組織，應用 establish 成立。

例句

The independent trade union was established by an international enterprise.

這獨立的商業公會是由一家國際企業所成立。

2. I can see your ~~worry~~ concern.

我能理解你的顧慮。

顧慮
☹worry
☺concern

"worry"表示一種持續的擔心狀況。例如：

Emily's loan problem is beginning to worry me.

（我很擔心 Emily 的貸款問題。）

但若是在面對選擇時，有所不同的考慮點，或是表達關心之意，則用

concern。

例句

John will attend the presentation tomorrow, but it's not our concern.

John 明天會參加發表會，但是這不是我們關心的重點。

Unit 6　慶功

Dialogue

Keith and Peter are in the bar
Keith跟Peter在酒吧

Peter　Keith, I'm glad that we finally reach an agreement. It's a good start of our cooperation. You don't have to worry about the import regulation. ☹ We have fully experience on South Africa import procedure. All you have to do is waiting in your warehouse, and then our tires will arrive soon.

Keith, 很高興我們達成協議了，這是我們合作的好開始。你不用擔心進口規定，我們在南非進口程序上有充分的經驗。你要做的就是在你們倉庫等著，然後我們的輪胎就會抵達了。

Keith　Great!! Last time, my container was held in customs detention for 2 months because we lacked of import documentation. The forfeit was USD$5,000, and that's not even the worst. My reputation was ruined, can you imagine that? It's totally a nightmare! You'd better keep your promise.

太好了！！上次我的貨櫃因為缺少進口文件而被海關扣留兩個月，罰款了 5000 美金。這還不算最糟的，我的公司信譽收損！！你能想像嗎？根本是場噩夢嘛。所以你最好說到做到。

Peter	I guarantee that everything will be fine. Remember Lion Product? They got their containers without a single problem.	我保證沒有問題，你記得 Lion 公司嗎？他們上次領櫃一點問題也沒有。
Keith	O.K. I trust you. We should open a bottle of wine for the new contract. What would you like to drink? I pay the bill.	好！我信你。我們該為了新合約開瓶酒，你想喝什麼，我請客。
Peter	I really appreciate that, but Juice is fine. I don't drink alcohol. It will make my face turn red.	謝謝你，但是我喝果汁就好。我沒辦法喝酒，一喝就臉紅。
Keith	Dude, <u>Are you serious</u>? You are in a bar, and you are a business man. In a bar, you talk to people, drink a little, it's fine. You should learn. Your company has party sometimes, right? People drink a little. If you don't, they may think you are too conservative.	老兄，你別開玩笑了。你在酒吧裡，而且你是商人。在酒吧裡，你跟人聊聊天，喝點小酒無妨的。你應該學學看，你們公司有時候會有派對吧，人們小酌一會。如果你都不喝，大家可能覺得你太保守了。

Part IV 其他

Peter	Alright, you are very persuasive. Maybe I can try. What are you suggesting?	好吧。你很有説服力。或許我可以試試看，你建議什麼比較好。
Keith	Well…I think beer is good enough for a starter.	嗯……我想對初學者來説啤酒就可以囉。
Bar tender	Good evening, what can I get for you?	晚安，要喝什麼？
Keith	Bourbon, please.	Bourbon 酒，謝謝。
Peter	Beer, and deep fried fish with fries, please.	啤酒，炸魚配薯條，謝謝。
Keith	Wow~ you skipped the dinner?	哇～你沒吃晚餐？
Peter	Yep, I was too busy in the exhibition. My booth was crowded with curious clients; they were very interested in our tire.	是呀，今天在展覽會場太忙了。我攤位上擠滿了好奇的顧客，大家對我們的輪胎很有興趣。
Keith	Good for you.	替你高興。

抓「龍」TIME

☹ We have fully experience on South Africa import procedure.
☺ We are fully experienced in South Africa import procedure.
☹ I pay the bill.
☺ It's my treat.

經典好用句

☺ **Are you serious?** 你是認真的嗎？不是開玩笑的吧？

A: Daryl is going to leave our team.
B: Are you serious? He is our best shooter.
A：Daryl 要離開我們隊伍了。
B：你不是開玩笑的吧，他是我們最好的射手。

☺ **Can you imagine**…? 你能想像……嗎？

A: Jenny is on diet, she haven't eaten anything for 2 days,
B: Wow ~ can you imagine that? Woman does crazy thing to keep fit.
A：Jenny 在節食，她兩天沒吃東西了。
B：哇，你能想像嗎？女生為了瘦身好瘋狂。

字彙精選

■ **lack of** *v* 缺少

Sally didn't get this job because lacking of related experiences.

因為缺乏相關經驗，Sally 並沒有得到這份工作。

■ **appreciate** *v* 感激；比"**Thank you**"再強烈的感謝之意

I really appreciate your kindness, but we have to leave today.

真的很感謝你的好意，但是我們今天就得離開。

■ **alcohol** *n* 酒

According to policy statistics, 2 main factors of car accident are speeding and drinking alcohol.

根據警方統計，車禍主要的原因為超速跟酒駕。

■ **conservative** *adj* 保守的

Wearing a bikini is quite impossible for conservative people.

對保守人士來說，是不可能穿比基尼泳裝的。

■ **persuasive** *adj* 有說服力的

Meredith made a persuasive argument, the client finally agreed with her.

Meredith 的說法很有說服力，客戶終於認同她。

■ **skip** *v* 略過，跳過

Carl skipped his class today; his parents got the phone call from his teacher.

Carl 今天翹課了，他父母接到老師的電話。

抓龍術大公開

1. We ~~have~~ are fully ~~experience on~~ experienced in South Africa import procedure.
   我們在南非進口程序上有充分的經驗。

   國人一般在遇到要說「有……」的時候，總是會直覺性地說出 have。
   而這一句常聽到的正確說法為"We are fully experienced in South Africa import procedure."。首先，先從 fully 來看，fully 是副詞，用以修飾動詞及形容詞，不能用來修飾名詞 experience。再來，如果是要說 have，則建議是說"have a full range of experiences"。

2. ~~I pay the bill~~ It's my treat.
   我付帳。

   字面上無誤，但是太直白了。但是有更好，也簡單的說法，正確為
   It's my treat!（我招待！）
   或是
   The drink is on me.（酒算我的，意思是我請客。）

 Unit 7 外出購物

Dialogue

Meredith, Christian, and April are in shopping center
Meredith、Christian和April在購物中心

Meredith	I need some eye cream; I have suffered from sleep deprivation.	我想買眼霜，我最近睡不太好。
Christian	I can tell that from your dark circles. What's bothering you?	妳的黑眼圈透露這個問題了，什麼事情讓妳煩心？
Meredith	Well, too much working pressure. I finished my report very late, and I kept thinking about it when I tried to sleep. My brain can't get rest.	工作壓力呀。我的報告很晚才完成，等我睡覺時，還是一直在想報告的事。我的腦袋根本沒辦法休息。
Christian	<u>Tell me about it.</u>	我也這麼認為。
Meredith	Excuse me, can you recommend some good eye cream for women in their late 20s?	請問，妳能推薦一些適合快 30 歲女生使用的眼霜嗎？

Clerk	Sure. This one would be perfect. It's got vitamin E and C to combat the first sign of aging.	這個就很適合，它有維他命 E 和 C 可以延緩初期老化現象。
Meredith	Does it help with dark circles? I have some sleep problems.	能消除黑眼圈嗎？我最近有點睡不好。
Clerk	Yes, it does.	可以的。
Meredith	Great, I'll take it. How do I use it?	太好了。那我要這個，要怎麼使用呢？
Clerk	Let me show you. You gently dab it under your eyes like this.	我示範給妳看，像這樣，輕輕點在眼睛下方即可。
Christian	Mer, maybe the eye cream could help, but the priority is you need to get some sleep.	小梅，或許眼霜可以讓妳的黑眼圈改善，但是最重要的是妳要好好睡覺。
Meredith	I know, I just want to do my best at Grey.	我知道，我只是想要把工作做好。
April	You should give yourself a break.	妳應該給自己喘口氣。
Meredith	Yes, I will, maybe after Jason's case. Come on, I also want to buy a foundation.	好～等我忙完 Jason 的案子，快走吧，我想買點粉底。

Meredith	It seems that I can't find a foundation color that's right for my skin.	我找不到適合我膚色的粉底。
Christian	What kind of foundation do you prefer? Cake or liquid?	妳想找哪種的，粉餅還是粉底液？
Meredith	I prefer liquid. But I want a natural look.	我比較想要粉底液，要自然膚色的。
Christian	Here, try this one. This one is very natural looking and would go well with your skin color. Try some on your cheek.	妳試試這個，看起來顏色很自然，而且跟妳膚色很襯，是在臉頰上。
Meredith	You are right. This one blends right in. Now we can go to H&M.	你說的沒錯，看不到色差。好啦，我們去 H&M。
April	Excuse me, do you know if there is an H&M in the mall.	請問，商場裡有 H&M 嗎？
Information	Yes, there is. Just go right from here, then make a right turn at the Gap, Keep following the corridor as it curves to the right, and H&M will be on your right.	有的，從這往右走，到 Gap 時候右轉。順著走道靠右，H&M 就在右手邊。
April	Ok, Thanks a lot.	好的，謝謝妳。

抓「龍」TIME

☹ How do I use it?

☺ How do I apply it?

☹ Would go well with your skin color.

☺ Would go well with your skin tone.

經典好用句

☺ **tell me about it!**　還用的著你說嗎！（意思是你說的都是事實，不是什麼新鮮事。請注意此句放在句尾時含意跟字義完全相反，並不是叫對方再多說一點的意思）

　　A: The construction noise is annoying; I can't sleep in the night.

　　B: Tell me about it.

　　A：工程的噪音真是煩人，晚上我都睡不好

　　B：還用的著你說嗎

☺ **give… a break**　給……喘個氣

　　You should give him a break, he is just a kid.

　　你應該給他喘口氣，他還是個小孩。

字彙精選

■ **deprivation**　*n*　喪失

　　Sleep deprivation is a serious problem; you should go to the doctor.

　　失眠是個嚴重的問題，你應該去看醫生。

Part IV 其他

■ **combat** *n/v* 搏鬥

It was the end of a long combat. People started to celebrate it.

這是一場長期戰鬥的結束，人們開始慶祝。

■ **dab** *v* 輕擦

The baby was crying, so the mother dabbed his eyes with a tissue.

小嬰兒一直哭，所以母親用面紙輕擦他的眼睛

■ **cheek** *v* 臉頰

The girl kissed her mom on the cheek and said "Goodbye".

小女孩在媽媽臉上親了一下，說聲再見。

■ **blend** *v* 融合

It's easy to make pudding, just blend in the milk, egg and some pudding powder.

做布丁很簡單的，只要將牛奶，雞蛋跟布丁粉混合即可。

■ **corridor** *n* 走道

You should not let your children running on the corridor. It's very dangerous.

你不該讓你小孩在走廊上奔跑，這樣很危險。

抓龍術大公開

1. How do I ~~use~~ apply it? 要怎麼用？

我要怎麼使用呢？

用
☹use
☺apply

在情境對話中，Meredith 詢問櫃姐眼霜要如何使用，這時我們應該使用
apply。

例句

Applying the lotion to your hand, it makes your hands softer.
擦點乳液在手上，你的皮膚會比較嫩。

2. Would go well with your skin ~~color~~ tone.
跟妳的膚色很襯

膚色
☹skin color
☺skin tone

雖然 skin color 也是指膚色，但代表的卻是不同人種的膚色，如黃種人、
黑人、白人的皮膚顏色。然而在西方國家，膚色是個敏感又複雜的問題。
須盡量避免用到 color 來形容人。所以在這裡要說 "skin tone" 色調。

例句

Emily choice of dress was a good match for her skin-tone.
Emily 選的洋裝很襯她的膚色。

Part IV 其他

· 289 ·

 Unit 8　在機場

 Dialogue

In the airport
在機場

Check-in Agent	Good evening, sir.	晚安，先生
Joseph	Good evening. I'd like to check in. My flight No. is CK201.	晚安，我想要報到，航班是 CK201。
Check-in Agent	<u>May I have</u> your passport, please.	麻煩請給我您的護照。
Check-in Agent	Yes, Mr. Joseph. Your flight is CK201 from Taipei to Amsterdam, then transfer to Copenhagen. And you had ordered the seafood meal on line.	有的，Mr. Joseph Chang，您的班機是 CK201 從台北飛阿姆斯特丹，再轉機到哥本哈根。您在網路上有預訂好海鮮餐了。
Joseph	That's correct. Can I get a window seat? I really like to look outside the window. It's an amazing scene.	是的，有靠窗的位置嗎？我很喜歡看窗外，景色很特別。

Check-in Agent	Sure, a window seat is arranged as your request. Did you pack your bags by yourself? Are there any batteries or cell phone inside your check-in luggage?	好的,靠窗位置安排好了。請問行李是您自己整理的嗎?托運行李裡面有電池或是手機嗎?
Joseph	Yes, I packed it myself, and I already took out the cell phone. I know there is a new regulation, no battery in the check-in luggage.	是我自己整理的,我已經將手機取出,我知道有個新規定,托運行李不能有電池。
Check-in Agent	Thank you, sir. How many bags would you like to check in?	謝謝您,您有幾件行李要托運呢?
Joseph	Just one bag, please. And I want to bring this small carry-on bag and my briefcase with me. Is that okay?	就這一件。我有一件小的隨身行李跟公事包要帶上飛機,可以吧?
Check-in Agent	Sure, no problem. And here are your passport and boarding pass. The boarding gate is No. 6, in the international terminal. Boarding time is at 11 PM. Enjoy your flight.	當然沒有問題,這是您的護照跟登機證,您的登機門是 6 號登機門,在國際航廈,登機時間晚上 11 點,祝您旅途愉快!

Part IV 其他

On the Airplane
在飛機上

| Joseph | I can't believe that I almost miss my flight. I spend too much time in the gift shop. There were crowded with people. It's too bad that I couldn't get any gift for my wife in time. She may be very disappointed. | 真不敢相信我差點錯過這班機。我花太多時間在免稅店了，那裡擠滿了人。真糟糕來不及幫我太太買禮物，她可能會很失望吶。 |

| Flight Attendant | Don't worry. We have tax-free goods on this flight. You can find the catalogue located in the seat-back pocket in front of you. There are various goods, I'm sure you will find something beautiful for your family. | 別擔心。飛機上有販賣免稅品，目錄放在您座位前方。裡面有各式各樣的商品，您一定可以為家人選些好禮物的。 |

| Joseph | Really? That's wonderful! Now I can finally rest assured. Can you bring me some Guava Juice? | 真的嗎？太好了。那我終於可以放心了，可以幫我倒點芭樂汁嗎？ |

| Flight Attendant | Sorry, we don't have Guava Juice, would you like to change apple juice. | 抱歉，飛機上沒有芭樂汁，蘋果汁好嗎？ |

| Joseph | Yes, please. | 好的，謝謝。 |

抓「龍」TIME

☹ We have tax-free goods on this flight.
☺ We have duty-free goods on this flight.
☹ Would you like to change apple juice?
☺ Would you like apple juice instead?

經典好用句

☺ **May I have**… 請給我…

以提問句的方式，客氣的表達自己的需求
May I have a glass of water, please?
請問可以給我一杯水嗎？

☺ **Enjoy your flight.** 祝搭機愉快。

Enjoy your… 可以做很多延伸，如
Enjoy your trip. 祝旅途愉快。
Enjoy your meal. 好好享受您的餐點。

字彙精選

■ **window seat & aisle seat** *n* 靠窗座位&靠走道座位

I prefer the aisle seat, it's easier to go to the bathroom without disturbing others people.

我比較喜歡靠走道的座位，可以比較方便去廁所而不打擾到其他旅客。

■ **regulation** *n* 規定

According to the hospital regulation, no visitor is allowed after 10 PM.

根據醫院的規定，晚上 **10** 點後訪客禁入。

■ **check-in & carry-on** 在這裡的解釋是托運行李跟隨身行李

I got 2 pieces of check-in luggage and 1 carry-on.

我有 **2** 間托運行李，一件手提行李。

■ **crowd with** 擠滿

The airport is crowded with tourists from around the world.

飛機場裡擠滿了來自世界各國的遊客。

■ **in time** 及時

We were lucky to catch up with the train in time.

我們很幸運的及時趕上火車。

■ **disappointed** *adj* 失望的

Without receiving Christmas gift, the Kid looked so disappointed.

沒有收到聖誕禮物，那小孩看來好失望。

■ **flight Attendant** *n* 空服員

The uniform of KLM's Flight attendant is blue.

荷蘭皇家航空的空服員制服是藍色的。

抓龍術大公開

1. We have ~~tax-free~~ duty-free goods on this flight.
   飛機上有販賣免稅品

   免稅品
   ☹tax-free goods
   ☺duty-free goods

   tax-free 與 duty-free 均可解釋成免稅，但是在其減少的稅上確有所差異，方式也不相同。tax-free 一般指的是免除消費稅的部分，在購買物品之後，需提出申請退稅。而 duty-free 則為免除關稅，免稅額較 tax-free 高，在購買時已經不含稅，不需再另外申請。在飛機上的免稅品範圍屬於 duty-free，而非 tax-free。

2. Would you like ~~to change apple juice~~ apple juice instead?
   您想要換成蘋果汁嗎？

   除了"change"之外，有時也會聽到有人說"Would you like to switch to apple juice?"，這樣的說法為中式英文。這時候可以用 instead adj 改為、替代，更為道地。

   例句

   > Kevin wanted to order Spaghetti, but he ordered rib instead.
   > Kevin 本來要點義大利麵的，但是他後來改點了豬肋排。

Part IV 其他

Unit 9　餐廳用餐

Dialogue

In the office
在辦公室

| Claire | It's been a long day, I'm glad ABC Company finally agreed with our proposal. We can inform the good news to Joseph right away. | 今天真是漫長，真高興 ABC 公司同意我們的提案了。我們馬上跟 Joseph 報告這個好消息了。 |

| Lawrence | Don't be silly. There's time difference it's 3 AM in Copenhagen. You don't want to wake up your boss at 3 AM. We can call Joseph couples hours later. I'm hungry. Let's go out and eat first. | 別傻了，有時差，哥本哈根現在早上 3 點。妳不會想在早上 3 點叫醒你的老闆吧！晚點再打給 Joseph，我餓死了，我們去吃點東西吧。 |

| Claire | You are right. I must be too excited to forget the time difference. We can call him after the dinner. Do you happen to know any good restaurant in the city? | 你說的對，我一定是太興奮忘了時差。我們吃完晚餐後再打電話好了，你知道市裡有什麼好餐廳嗎？ |

Lawrence	Hum. The boy in the hotel lobby told me that there is a good restaurant nearby. It's called "Opera", only 2 blocks away. We can walk by.	飯店大廳的服務員跟我說這附近有間餐廳不錯叫"Opera"。離這裡 2 條街就到了，我們可以走路去。
Claire	"Opera". I know it. It's easy to remember. I read it in a travel guide. It says " Can't be missed". Let's go!!	Opera ？我聽過這家餐廳，名字很好記吶。我在旅遊指南讀過，指南上寫"不可錯過的好味道"。我們走吧。

In the restaurant
在餐廳中

Waitress	Good night, I'm Judy. What would you like to order?	晚安，我是 Judy，想吃些什麼？
Claire	Everything looks delicious on the menu, so many choices, is there anything that you want to recommend?	菜單上的食物看起來都好美味，有好多選擇。有什麼推薦的嗎？
Waitress	Would you like to try our Today's special. It's crawfish spaghetti with borscht. The crawfish is very fresh today.	要試試我們今天的特餐嗎？是小龍蝦義大利麵跟羅宋湯，今天的小龍蝦很新鮮。

Part IV 其他

Claire	Sounds Great!! I would take that.	聽起來很不錯,那我要一份特餐。
Waitress	OK, one Today's special for the lady. And you, sir?	好的,一份特餐給女士。先生,您要什麼呢?
Lawrence	I'm allergic to seafood. I want a cheese burger and chicken salad; can I have salad dressing on the side?	我對海鮮過敏,給我一份起司漢堡跟雞肉沙拉,可以幫我把沙拉醬分開嗎?
Waitress	Absolutely! Your meals will be ready soon.	沒問題,您們的餐點很快就好了。

Phone rings··· Claire's on the phone
電話響,Claire電話中

Claire	I can't eat now!!	我吃不下了!!
Lawrence	What happened? Who's on the phone?	怎麼了,剛剛在跟誰講電話?
Claire	It's Lucy from ABC Company. They want to cancel the order.	是 ABC 公司 的 Lucy,她說要取消訂單……

抓「龍」TIME

☹ Good night.
☺ Good evening.
☹ I can't eat now.
☺ I just lost my appetite.

經典好用句

☺ **it's been a long day** 真是漫長的一天

通常在忙碌一整天之後，人們常用這句。

It's been a long day. I really need some rest. I won't be in office tomorrow.

今天真是忙壞了，我需要好好休息。明天不進辦公室了。

☺ **don't be silly** 別傻了

在形容對方有點傻氣，說話不切實際。.

Don't be silly. Marvin will never give up on his position, no matter how hard he promised you.

別傻了，不論 Marvin 怎麼跟你保證的，他才不會放棄他的職位。

字彙精選

■**inform** *v* 通知

The telephone company just informed us that our bill is overdue.

電信公司剛剛通知我們說帳單到期了。

Part IV 其他

■ **time difference**　時差

There is an hour's time difference between Tokyo and Taipei.
東京跟台北有一個小時的時差。

■ **excited** *adj*　興奮的

I'm very excited about Apple's new product launch
tomorrow; I can't wait to see the new iPhone.
對於明天的蘋果新品發表會，我感到很興奮，等不及想看看新的 iPhone
了。

■ **recommend** *v*　推薦

Judy recommended Francis to be our new English teacher.
Judy 推薦 Francis 當我們的新英文老師。

■ **allergic** *adj*　過敏

Many people are allergic to peanuts; therefore the Airlines
consider to stop offering the small snack.
許多人對花生過敏，因此航空公司考慮不再提供這類小點心。

■ **absolutely** *adj*　絕對的，十分的

A: Are you sure that Lisa won't come to our branch office in
　London on February 15?
B: Absolutely! She told me in the face and she will be in
　Seattle then.
A：你確定 Lisa 二月十五日不會去我們的 London 分公司嗎？
B：當然！！她當面告訴我的，而且那時候她就已經在 Seattle 了。

抓龍術大公開

1. Good ~~night~~ evening!!
晚安！！

晚安（見面時）
☹Good night.
☺Good evening.

晚上打招呼時，請不要再用"Good night."，中式英文中常出現的早安，午安，晚安－good morning，good afternoon，good evening/night。其中，Good night 應該是晚上要離開或要睡覺休息時才用，而在晚上見面時，應說 good evening。用了 good night，則是表示要離開……請大家不要再搞混了。
當我們晚上遇到某人，或剛進教室時，打招呼正確用法為：
Good evening, everyone, welcome to the class.
晚安，各位，歡迎來上課。

2. I ~~can't eat now~~ just lose my appetite!!
我吃不下了

沒胃口
☹can't eat
☺lose appetite

appetite　n　胃口，食慾
例句

When seeing the dead fish, I just lost my appetite.
一看到死魚，我就沒胃口吃飯了。

Unit 10 搭乘火車

Dialogue

Jack and Ivan are taking the train to Stockholm
Jack跟Ivan搭乘火車前往斯德哥爾摩

Jack	Good morning, two go and return tickets to Stockholm, with the registered seat. This is my credit card.	我要兩張去斯德哥爾摩的來回票，對號座。信用卡在這。
Clerk	Ok, please enter your pin code.	好，請輸入密碼。
Jack	No problem.	沒問題。
Clerk	Here are your tickets and credit card. The train no. is CK508, track 5, at 8:30 AM.	這是你的票跟信用卡，火車編號 CK508，5 號月台，早上 8:30。
Jack	Here we are. Track 5. Let me check the timetable.	五號月台，我們到了。我看一下時刻表。
Ivan	What's our schedule today?	我們今天行程怎麼安排。

Jack	Well, we shall arrive in Stockholm about 2PM, then head to the client's office directly by taxi. You know, Mr. Henk said "Please be punctual for the meeting" in the email. So, it would be better if we can be there on time.	我們應該下午 2 點左右到斯德哥爾摩，然後直接坐計程車去客戶辦公室。你知道上次 Henk 信裡說"會議請務必準時"，所以我們最好不要遲到。
Jack	Where are our seats? 90A, 90B. Excuse us; I think you are in my seat.	我們的位置在哪裡？90A，90B。 抱歉，我想你坐到我的位置了。
A	Sorry.	抱歉。
Jack	Ivan, over here ~	Ivan，這邊。
Ivan	Finally ~Let me put the baggage on the upper rack. We should get some sleep, so we can save some energy for the conference this afternoon.	終於找到了，我把行李放到上面架子上。我們最好睡一會，留點體力下午才有精神開會。
Jack	You bet!!	當然

Broadcast	Ladies and gentlemen, due to the bad weather, our arrival time will be delayed 20 minutes. We are sorry for the inconvenience; our dinning car is in the no.7.	女士先生們，因為天氣不佳，我們的到達時間將會晚 20 分鐘。很抱歉造成您的不便。餐車在七號車廂。
Jack	Hey, Ivan, I am thirty. I am going to get a drink, do you need anything?	Ivan，我口渴，去餐車喝點東西。你要什麼嗎？
Ivan	Thanks, I'm good. I'll look our baggage on the rack.	謝謝，不用了。我在這看著行李。
Conductor	Sir, may I see your ticket, please.	先生，我可以看一下你的票嗎？
Ivan	Oh ~ my friend has it! He just went to the dining car, I'm sure he will be back in any minute. There he is. Jack, the tickets!	哦，放在我朋友那裡，他去餐車了。他馬上就回來，來了。Jack！查票了。
Jack	Here are the tickets; I heard that the arrival time will be delayed, the train is decelerating?	票在這，我聽說抵達時間會延誤。火車在減速啊？

| Conductor | Yes, it is. The snow was falling heavily this morning, for the safety reason. We need to slow down, but I'm sure the delay won't exceed 20 minutes. | 是的，早上的下了場大雪，為了安全我們得減速。但是我很確定延誤不會超過 20 分鐘。 |

抓「龍」TIME

☹ Two go and return tickets to Stockholm.
☺ Two round trip tickets to Stockholm.
☹ I'll look our baggage on the rack.
☺ I'll keep an eye on our baggage on the rack.

經典好用句

☺ **it would be better**　最好是……

It would be better to inform your parents about your absence this morning.

你早上缺席了，我們最好通知你的父母。

☺ **I think you are in my seat**　我想你坐到我的座位了

要提醒對方時，前面加上"I think"有緩和語氣之意。

A: Excuse me; I think you are in my seat.
B: Oops, I'm sorry.

A：打擾了，你坐到我的座位了。
B：糟了，抱歉。

字彙精選

■ **registered seat** *n* 對號座

Jack paid extra fare for the registered seat.

Jack 付了額外的車費而得到了對號座。

■ **pin code** *n* 密碼

Travelling in Europe, you need a pin code for the credit card.

在歐洲旅遊時,你需要密碼才能使用信用卡。

■ **punctual** *adj* 嚴格準時的

Rick is a reliable and punctual person. Everyone trusts him.

Rick 是個可靠,準時的人。大家都很信任他。

■ **energy** *n* 精神,力氣,能源

Nuclear Energy is a dispute for many countries.

許多國家對核能爭議不休。

■ **thirty** *adj* 口渴

The baby is crying loudly, he is thirty.

嬰兒哭的很響亮,他口渴了。

■ **decelerate** *v* 減速,降低

The government has made every effort to decelerate the unemployment rate.

政府盡全力以降低失業率。

抓龍術大公開

1. Two ~~go and return~~ round-trip tickets to Stockholm.
兩張去斯德哥爾摩的來回票。

來回票
☹go and return ticket
☺round trip ticket

單程票為 **one way ticket**；回程票為 **round trip ticket**

2. I'll look our baggage on the rack.
我在這看著行李。

看照行李
☹look our baggage
☺keep an eye on our baggage

keep an eye on 看照

例句

Can you please keep an eye on the stove? I need to answer this phone.
幫我看著爐上的火好嗎？我得接這電話。

Part IV 其他

Unit 11
招待客戶－晚餐

Dialogue

Ivan, Jack, and Henk are in the Stockholm restaurant
Ivan、Jack和Henk在一家斯德哥爾摩餐廳

Jack	This is a good restaurant, Henk, a nice atmosphere, pleasant decoration and a polite service. Do you come here often?	Henk，這餐廳不錯。氣氛很好，裝潢時尚，服務很周到。你常來嗎？
Henk	Once in a while, my wife and I love this restaurant. They have a wide variety of dishes from different European and North American style. All of these dishes are very popular. I'm sure you can enjoy your dinner here.	偶而，我太太跟我都還蠻喜歡這餐廳的。他們的菜色很多樣，從歐洲菜到北美菜色都有。所有的菜色都很受歡迎，你們一定不會失望的。
Ivan	Seems they've chosen their location wisely as well, right downtown, in the business district.	看來他們地點選的很好吶，在市中心，又是商業區。

Henk	Actually, the owner is my father's brother's son. Sorry, my English is very bad. Anyway, one of my relatives owns this restaurant. He was a fish man, 5 years ago; he decided to open a restaurant. He got a loan from the bank and started to make his plan come true.	事實上，老闆是我父親兄弟的兒子。抱歉，我的英文不好。總之，是我親戚的開的。他本來是個漁夫，五年前，他決定開餐廳。他跟銀行貸款，開始實現他的計畫。
Odur	Hi, Henk. What brings you here today? I haven't seen you for a while.	嘿，Henk，你怎麼在這裡？有陣子沒看到你了。
Henk	Hi, Odur. These are my guests from Asia, Jack and Ivan. They are in town for the business.	嘿 Odur，這兩位是我亞洲的客人，Jack 和 Ivan，他們來談生意。
Odur	Nice to meet you. I'm Odur, Henk's cousin, the restaurant owner. Henk, you look better than ever. All the drinks are on the house tonight. I hope you and your guests have a wonderful evening. Enjoy your dinner.	很榮幸見到你們。我是 Odur，Henk 的表弟，餐廳的老闆。Henk 你看起來不錯吶，今天的飲料都算我的。我希望你和你的客人晚餐能夠盡興，好好享受。

Part IV 其他

Henk	Thanks. I'll talk to you later.	謝謝你。我們晚點聊。
Ivan	Henk, Your cousin is very generous.	Henk，你表弟很大方呀。
Henk	Yes, he is. I haven't seen him for a while. I heard he was travelling. Listen, what is your plan for this weekend?	是呀，我有一陣子沒看到他了，聽說他去旅行了。你們週末計畫做什麼呢？
Jack	Since we already made a formal agreement about the exclusive agency. Ivan and I were thinking about go to the Skansen Open-Air Museum.	既然我們的代理合約都談好了。Ivan 跟我想說去 Skansen 露天博物館。
Henk	You should!! This is the oldest open-air museum in the world; it shows the traditional Scandinavia life style. There are historical buildings and dwellings. People in period dress. Oh ~ and the wolves.	那裏值得一去。它是世界上最古老的露天博物館，展示傳統斯堪地半島的生活樣貌，有古老的建築物，跟住所，穿著舊式衣服的人。對了，還有狼。

抓「龍」TIME

☹ My English is very bad.
☺ My English is not good.
☹ He decided to open a restaurant.
☺ He decided to run a restaurant.

經典好用句

☺ **you look better than ever**　你看起來不錯

遇見朋友打招呼時，所使用的問候句。
Leo, you look better than ever.
Leo，你看起來氣色不錯。

☺ **make something come true**　使……成真

After 10 years hard working, he finally has made his dream come true.
經過 10 年的努力工作，他的夢想終於成真。

字彙精選

■**atmosphere**　*n*　氣氛
Under the romantic atmosphere, many people fall in love in Paris.
在浪漫的氣氛下，許多人在巴黎陷入熱戀。

Part IV 其他

■ **decoration** *n* 裝潢

Leo is a realistic person. He won't spend too much money on the new house decoration.
Leo 是個很務實的人，他不會在新房的裝修上花費太多。

■ **loan** *n* 借款

They got a loan from West bank last week, and planned to buy a new car.
他們上星期跟西方銀行借了一筆錢，打算買新車。

■ **generous** *adj* 大方的，慷慨的

Their boss is very generous and he just denated 2 million dollars to charity.
他們老闆很慷慨，剛捐了二百萬給慈善機構。

■ **exclusive agency** *n* 獨家代理權

After 2 months negotiation, Inno finally agreed to lease the exclusively agency to VASA.
經過 2 個月的談判，Inno 終於同意將代理權放給 Vasa。

■ **dwellings** *n* 住所

He has a dwelling in Hong Kong.
他在香港有一處住所。

抓龍術大公開

1. My English is ~~very bad~~ not good. 我的英文很不好
   形容英文程度不好

   ☹very bad
   ☺not good

受到中文思考的影響，我們會直接說出如對話中這樣的句子，或是過份謙虛的貶低自己的英文程度而說"My English is poor."。這樣的說法在文法上並沒有錯，但是卻不太符合英文上的常用說法。外國人一般在說明自己的外語程度時，通常會以較積極的態度來回應，例如：

My Mandarin is pretty basic. （我的中文只能講點基礎的。）
I am still having some problem, but I think I'm getting better.
（我還有些小問題，但我覺得我有在進步了。）
所以，請記得下次在回答覺得自己的英文不夠好時，如果想要有點謙虛，也想說得道地，就請說"My English is not good enough."囉！

2. He decided to ~~open~~ run a restaurant.
他決定開餐廳。

經營餐廳
☹ open a restaurant
☺ run a restaurant

在對話當中得知 Odur 已經開餐廳開 5 年了，所以這裡的「開餐廳」應該是指「經營餐廳」，而開餐廳＝經營餐廳，則是中文才有的說法，請不要直譯哦。在英文裡，用到 open 表示為開幕，所以 open a restaurant，通常指的是準備一家餐廳要開張前所有事項的工作。而經營一間餐廳則要用 run。

例句

Adam runs a famous restaurant in downtown.
Adam 在市中心開了間有名的餐廳。

Part IV 其他

Unit 12
招待客戶 - 博物館

Ivan	Jack, wake up, <u>rise and shine</u>. Why you didn't pick up the phone? We are going to the Skansen Museum this morning. Henk just lined me; he would meet us in the hotel lobby.	Jack 起床了，天都亮了。你幹嘛不接電話。我們要去 Skansen 博物館。Henk 剛發訊息給我，他在飯店大廳跟我們碰面。
Jack	Sorry, my cellphone has no power. I'll get myself ready in 10 minutes.	抱歉，我手機沒電了。我十分鐘準備好出門。
Ivan	Morning, Henk. It's nice to have your company.	早，Henk，很高興今天你跟我們一起去
Henk	Well, <u>I hope that you don't mind</u> that my son is joining us. Actually, he has learned Chinese in the college for a year. Last night, I mentioned about my Asia guests. He almost begged me to let him join us.	希望你們不要介意，我兒子也想跟我們一起去。事實上他修過一年中文課。昨天，我提到了我的亞洲客人，他幾乎是求我帶他一起來。

Ivan	Of course not. I would like that.	當然，沒問題，我很歡迎。
Henk	It's my son, Tiw, this Jack, and Ivan.	這是我兒子，Tiw，這二位是 Jack 跟 Ivan。
Jack	Nice to meet you, Tiw. I heard that you studied Chinese in the college?	很高興認識你，Tiw，聽說你在學校學中文？
Tiw	Yes, Sir. My major is Chinese Architecture. Kind of wierd, right? When I was a little boy, I read "Alone on the Great Wall", the writer is an Englishman William Lindesay. For some unexplainable reasons, I'm fascinated with Chinese stuff; it's a mysterious and faraway place. One day, I hope I can visit Zhou Zhuang. That's my love most place.	是的，先生。我主修是中國建築，有點奇怪吧。當我小時候，讀過一本英國人 William Lindesay 寫的「獨征長城」。有種無法解釋的理由，我對中國的東西很著迷，那是個神祕又遙遠的地方。有天，我想去周莊看看，那是我最喜歡的地方。
Jack	That's a very famous historical town, if my memory is correct. That town was built 1,000 year ago, surrounded by water, and still retains its old character. It's a very attractive town.	那是個很有名的歷史景點。如果我沒記錯的話，那小城建於 1,000 年前，四面環水，維持著舊式建築的特色，十分迷人的小鎮。

Part IV 其他

Tiw	I am saving money for my Asia trip next year. May I have your contact, sir? I hope you can give me some advice about my trip.	我正在為我明年的亞洲行存錢。先生,能給我您的聯絡方式嗎?或許您可以給我一些旅行的建議。
Jack	Sure thing. Here is my email; let's keep in touch.	沒問題,這是我的電子信箱,讓我們保持聯絡。
Henk	It looks that you've made a new friend.	看來你交了新朋友。
Ivan	Henk, would you consider going to Asia with Tiw next year?	Henk,那你明年會考慮跟 Tiw 一起去亞洲嗎?
Henk	Well, we are not sure about it yet. But if I do, I definitely will visit you.	嗯,我們還不是很確定。如果我去的話,一定去拜訪你們。

抓「龍」TIME

☹ My cellphone has no power.
☺ My cellphone is dead.
☹ That's my love most place.
☺ That's my favorite place.

經典好用句

☺ **rise and shine**　天亮了，快起來

十分口語的英文，叫對方起床，表示今日又是美好的一天

A: Rise and shine, we are going to picnic today.

B: I thought it's raining.

A：起床了，天氣這麼好。我們今天要去野餐。

B：我以為還在下雨呢。

☺ **I hope that you don't mind**…　我希望你不要介意

A: I was hungry. I don't that you don't mind I ate your sandwich.

B: Don't worry; I already had lunch with Owen.

A：我剛餓了，所以吃掉你的三明治，希望你不要介意。

B：沒關係啦，我剛跟 Owen 吃過午餐。

字彙精選

■ **company**　*n*　陪伴

這裡 company 的意思不是公司，而是陪伴。

We are grateful for your company in the Europe trip.

歐洲行有你們的陪伴，我們十分感謝。

■ **architecture** *n* 建築

Jack studies architecture in the college, but he turns out to be an engineer.

Jack 在大學學的是建築，但是他最後成為了工程師。

■ **unexplainable** *adj* 無法解釋的

For some unexplainable reasons, Maggie left home. We can't find her.

不知什麼原因，Maggie 離家出走了，我們找不到她。

■ **fascinate** *v* 著迷，入迷

Owen is so fascinated with Lego.

Owen 對 Lego（樂高）十分著迷。

■ **faraway** *adj* 遙遠的，偏遠的

Many elders don't like to travel faraway places. They rather stay at home.

許多年長者並不喜歡到遠地方旅行，他們寧願待在家裡。

■ **surround** *v* 環繞，包圍

The small village is surrounded by mountains, therefore, it's isolated for hundreds years.

小村莊被山脈圍繞著，因此好幾百年來與世隔絕。

抓龍術大公開

1. My cellphone ~~has no power~~ is dead.

我手機沒電了。

沒電了（手機）
☹has no power
☺is dead

説手機沒電最常用的英文説法就是"My cellphone is dead."，在這裡的 dead 指的跟死亡沒關係，而是指手機因為沒電而沒有反應。如果要説電池的部分則可以説"My battery is dead."。快要沒電了則是"My battery is running low."。手機沒電還有一種俏皮的説法就是"My cellphone is out of juice."，這裡的 juice 指的不是果汁，而是在英文俚語中的"power"（電力）的意思。

例句

A: Why you didn't call me back yesterday?
B: Sorry, my phone was dead.
A：你昨晚怎麼不回電給我？
B：抱歉，我手機沒電了。

2. That's my ~~love most~~ favorite place
那是我最愛的地方

最喜愛
☹love most
☺favorite

如果一定要用 love most 的話，那應該改説成"That's the place I love most."。"favorite"在這裡做形容詞，做「最喜愛的」解釋。在形容最喜歡的地方時，可説 favorite place。

例句

Maroon 5 is my favorite band.
Maroon 5 是我最愛的樂團。

Learn Smart! 047

90 關鍵英語烏龍句之高效抓「龍」術，職場溝通不 NG！

作　　者　Jessica Su
封面構成　高鍾琪
內頁構成　華漢電腦排版有限公司

發 行 人　周瑞德
企劃編輯　陳欣慧
校　　對　陳韋佑、饒美君
印　　製　大亞彩色印刷製版股份有限公司
初　　版　2015 年 06 月
定　　價　新台幣 360 元
出　　版　倍斯特出版事業有限公司
電　　話　(02) 2351-2007
傳　　真　(02) 2351-0887
地　　址　100 台北市中正區福州街 1 號 10 樓之 2
E - m a i l　best.books.service@gmail.com

港澳地區總經銷　泛華發行代理有限公司
地址　香港筲箕灣東旺道 3 號星島新聞集團大廈 3 樓
電話　(852) 2798-2323
傳真　(852) 2796-5471

國家圖書館出版品預行編目(CIP)資料

90 關鍵英語烏龍句之高效抓「龍」術，職場
溝通不 NG！ / Jessica Su 著. -- 初版. -- 臺北
市：倍斯特, 2015.06
　面　；　公分. -- (Learn smart! ; 47)
ISBN 978-986-91915-0-0(平裝)

1.英語 2.職場 3.讀本

805.18　　　　　　　　　　104009261